The Private Tutor

AJ Carter

Copyright © 2024 by Papyrus Publishing LTD.
All rights reserved. No part of this publication may be reproduced, distributed, or transmitted in any form or by any means, including photocopying, recording, or other electronic or mechanical methods, without the prior written permission of the publisher, except in the case of brief quotations embodied in critical reviews and certain other non-commercial uses permitted by copyright law. For permission requests, write to the publisher, addressed "Attention: Permissions Coordinator," at the address below.

contact@ajcarterbooks.com

Dedication

For my daughter, who inspires everything I do.

And for my dog, who farts in her sleep.

The Private Tutor

Prologue

In the race for my life, I climb out onto the roof. There's a voice behind me, shrill and desperate as it barks at me to get back inside and take what's coming to me. Obeying that order would mean certain death, so I take my chances in the freezing open air.

The wind whips at my head. I find Jacob on the tiles next to me, his fragile little six-year-old fingers grasping onto the guttering for dear life. I take his hands and tell him to trust me – that it's all going to be okay if only he will let me take care of him.

Yes, I lie to him.

Behind us, their shadow occupies the window, the rifle unable to reach us because of the obscured angle. We're not safe here – we could die at any moment, if not from a gunshot, then from the fall. The ground below, although grassy and moist from the melted snow, is so far away that the fall is likely to kill us. But it's still safer than staying up here with them.

This can only mean one thing.

We have to jump.

I lead Jacob towards the end of the roof, standing behind him and watching his balance. He fully trusts me to lead him there safely, the icy wind taking our breath away. When we reach the edge, there's a long leap to the nearest low roof of the garage. I stand there, sweating despite the cold, measuring the distance with nothing but sight. My heart sinks when I realise.

I'm not sure we can make it.

'Do we have to jump?' Jacob whines over the fierce night-time wind.

'Maybe.'

Glancing back at the window, I can only see the rifle perched over the edge. It's clear what they're doing now: they're watching the main gate and patiently awaiting their chance to kill me from afar. It's great that there's no room for them to pivot the weapon, but as soon as we make it down to the ground – *if* we make it down – there's still that to contend with.

'All right,' I tell Jacob, slowly kneeling to meet his beady, vulnerable little eyes. I understand his fear because I feel it myself. Even more than the harsh, unforgiving cold of this ice-cold night, the terror is seeping into my bones. 'Here's what we're going to do...'

Chapter One

My very first moment in Wedchester comes with a shock. It's not the fact that I'm alone in this small, close-knit community. It's not even the fact it's gone midday and I don't have any accommodation. It's the cold that hits me where it hurts, piercing through my numb skin and seizing my bones from the second I step off the bus.

I shouldn't be surprised, really. January is the coldest month of the year in England, and this northern town has a reputation for getting more snow and ice than anywhere else in the country. It's enough to make me regret coming here in the first place, but I had to see what all the fuss is about – it appears in every 'Top 10 Places' book I've read, and I'm between jobs at the moment anyway. In short, there's been no better time for me to wander.

The bus doors close, and it hisses before taking off. I'm stranded on the edge of a town that, from the looks of things, I could walk from one end to the other in about ten minutes. I'm trying to decide if that should make it more or less difficult to secure accommodation.

Regardless, I pull up the handle on my suitcase and begin my careful descent from the hill while praying I don't slip and land on my perfect little arse (I'm not vain; I'm just quoting what many men have told me). Wedchester looks beautiful at first glance, the midday sun bouncing off the ice that's settled on the hilly roads. It makes the town look as though it's made of crystal, which would make for a magnificent postcard if those were still popular.

By the time I reach the town proper, my nose is running, and I can't feel my cheeks. Multiple people pass me, each one beaming and nodding or wishing me a good afternoon as if we've been friends for years. I can't figure out if it makes me feel like a tourist – a foreigner in an unknown land that's welcoming people from the outside world – or like one of them. It's a warm, inviting feeling I never expected to stumble across.

The streets are narrow, the roads even more so. Only two cars have passed during my entire walk, which I guess makes sense because the residents of this town don't need to drive – everything is within walking distance, and they probably keep their cars locked up for when they want to leave town. At least, that's my theory.

When I finally find the high street, I'm amazed to find it buzzing with life. More hellos come from the young and old alike, each of them coming out of or going into one of the many establishments: a pub, a charity shop, two small supermarkets that look more sanitary than anywhere I've ever seen, a bookshop, and a café. That's what I can see from where I stand on the edge of the pavement, but the street goes on further. I'll explore more of that later, but right now, I need to focus on letting some blood run through my toes before they fall off and getting hold of a tissue so I can finally blow my nose and not look like some kid's drawing of Shrek's pink cousin. This means I need warmth, and I'll get it from the nearest source available.

In this case, it's the café that grabs my attention.

. . .

A BELL above the door dings as I enter. Heads turn to look at me, and half the conversations die immediately. I stand there awkwardly, feeling like a cowboy who just entered the saloon and is about to get confronted by someone mean and scary. The more I examine the faces, the less comfortable I feel. The sea of scowls tells me these people aren't nearly as welcoming as the people out in the street. But then I realise why.

I'm letting all the cold air in.

'Sorry,' I say, rushing to pull my suitcase off the step so I can close the door.

The chatter continues, which makes me feel a little more comfortable. To be honest, I'm just glad to be in a nice, warm room. I can feel the cold falling off me. It's like ice sliding off a frozen chicken as it thaws. Nothing has ever felt so good.

I order a coffee from the woman at the counter, and she tells me to take a seat. She doesn't have to tell me twice. Although my body is aching from the long bus ride from Bristol, where I took my last temp job that lasted all of two weeks, my legs have turned to jelly from the assault of cold weather. I'm only thirty-six, and my knees should not be hurting this much. They even click as I sit down, which only proves they needed the break.

The sofa in the corner is comfortable, but I'm only sitting for a few seconds before spotting the noticeboard. Back onto my feet I go, hurrying to examine the ads and praying for a job of some kind. There are local events for charities and something about a bench for a local politician who died, but otherwise, it's all just cleaning services and party hosts. It appears there's not a single job in this town.

Much less a place to stay.

A huge mug reaches the coffee table just as I sit back down. The waitress smiles at me, her youthful features a far cry from the old crow who served me at the counter. I thank her as I eyeball the enormous mug and the biscuit sitting beside it, only now noticing my hunger.

'Do you serve food?' I ask before she can run off.

'Absolutely. Would you like to see a menu?'

'If you do full English breakfasts, that's good enough for me.'

The waitress smiles, tucks her hair over one ear, then clicks out a pen and scribbles down my order. As she writes, she briefly glances at my suitcase, then meets my eye. 'New in town, are you? Moving in or just passing through?'

I shrug. 'Depends if there's enough reason to stay. I'm looking for work.'

'Oh? What kind of work?'

'Well, I'm a teacher, but I'll take anything at this point.'

'Hmm. Nothing on the noticeboard?'

'Nope.'

'That's a shame.' She heaves a sigh. 'Well, one full English coming right up.'

After thanking the waitress, I sit forward and grab the mug in both hands. The warmth defrosts my palms, the feeling quickly returning to my fingers. I inhale, soaking up the smell of coffee after a long, arduous journey. My stomach groans, reminding me that food is on the way. It's the only thing about my future that's certain.

'Excuse me,' comes a frail voice from somewhere to my left.

I scan the room to see who spoke, then find a small, elderly woman sitting on a nearby table. She's almost hanging off her chair to talk to me. The man sitting across from her – possibly her husband – rolls his eyes and goes back to reading his book. I'm guessing the woman has a habit of talking to strangers that doesn't sit right with him.

'Did I overhear that you're looking for work?' she asks.

'Yes, that's right.' I put the mug down like it weighs a ton.

'And you're a teacher?'

'When I'm employed, yes.'

Something curious happens then. She looks to the man across from her, who looks up from his book only long enough to shake his head disapprovingly, his frown not budging so much as an inch. The woman hesitates, examines her nails while appearing deep in thought, then finally turns back to me. Needless to say, my suspicions are sufficiently aroused.

'There is one job I know of,' she says. 'A lovely couple that lives on the hill need a private tutor for their young boy. They're having trouble filling the position, so there would be no competition as long as you're qualified.'

My jaw almost drops. Luck has always had a way of overlooking me, but now that it's noticed, it's making up for lost time. I scoot along the sofa to get closer to the old woman, just so I can hear her better over the puffs of steam coming from the nearby kitchen. She rotates her body in the wooden chair, ready to tell me more.

'Where are you from, young lady?' she asks.

'London originally. But I just came from Bristol.'

'Lovely. I always wanted to visit Bristol.'

All I can do is smile as she continues.

'Well, I'm told the job will pay well. The parents have become very desperate since their last tutor... left town. If you head up to their house and introduce yourself, I'm almost certain they'll welcome you with open arms.'

'That's great. Where exactly do they live?'

'In the Hill House.'

I tilt my head to one side, lost.

'Didn't you see it when you came into town? There's a big white house sitting at the top of the hill. It's quite a walk up there, and I wouldn't recommend taking the journey by foot. Especially with your luggage.' She points at my suitcase without looking. 'Try taking a taxi.'

There's no explanation as to how I missed a massive white house on the top of a hill, but perhaps I was just distracted by the cold. It's like this whenever I enter unfamiliar terrain – I get distracted by the many sights to take in all at once and can't see it all in a single look. Not that it matters. Work is work, and I may have just found something perfect for me.

There's only one thing that concerns me: the way she spoke of the previous tutor. Try as I might, it was hard to ignore the woman's husband as she explained they'd left town. No matter how brief, his hand definitely came away from his book as if to stop her from sharing more. I wanted to ask, of course, but there's an old saying about looking a gift horse in the mouth.

Still, the way she said it left me feeling incredibly uncomfortable.

"Their last tutor... left town."

THE TAXI TAKES me straight up the hill, struggling to find purchase on the icy road. The driver – bless him and his thick northern accent that makes it difficult to understand much of what he's saying – grumbles as the car slides all over the place. It takes longer than it should to reach the house, and in hindsight, it probably wasn't the safest journey in the world.

I pay the driver and ask him to wait until I'm inside, then turn to look up at a house that's only a few small rooms away from being a mansion. The brick is as white as the ice on its front path. The surrounding grounds stretch on so far that it would take ages to walk alongside the wall that surrounds them. The entire property looks like it was plucked out of a Victorian novel and then modernised with double glazing and marble pillars. *Marble.* Just how much money does this married couple have?

The driver kills his engine. There's not a sound on this hill besides the howling wind that's blowing my hair all over the place. He nods at me as if encouraging me to hurry the hell up, and I quickly oblige by opening the creaky gate and wandering towards the front door. Not knowing who or what to expect, I press the doorbell and wait in the silence. The pillars break the wind, so at least I'm out of harm's way while I wait with a sudden bout of anxiety.

What if the people don't like me? What if I don't like them? My background in teaching is enough to put me in their good graces, but how might these people react to a stranger standing on their doorstep and asking for a job?

The door swings open then.

It's time to find out.

Chapter Two

THE WOMAN who greets me is nothing like how I pictured her. When looking at a house like this, I half expected to see a wealthy woman with pearls around her neck, perfect hair that's fresh from the salon, and a demeanour that speaks down to all those beneath her.

What I get is the polar opposite.

She's about my age, but she'd probably look younger if it weren't for the black, weighted bags under her eyes. She's painfully thin, her bones poking so far from her skin it's like they're about to burst through. Her blonde hair, although short and relatively tidy, is frayed and discoloured, the first signs of grey peeking from the roots of her blonde dye.

Then there are the eyes. Not cold, not judgemental, and certainly not condescending. They seem to match her voice when she asks me who I am and what I'm doing on her property. Not because she hates to see an intruder on her doorstep, but because she needs the company.

Because she's afraid.

'I'm so sorry to drop in on you like this,' I say, suddenly noticing how dry my mouth is. 'My name is Emma Corbin. I'm new in town and heard there might be a vacancy for a tutoring position. I was wondering if we might be able to talk a little?'

The woman, whose name I still don't know, examines me from head to toe. I stand there uncomfortably, her eyes roaming over my entire body as if she's Sherlock Holmes using his famous Science of Deduction. The female version, of course. Then, her gaze drops to my luggage, and I think I know what's running through her mind.

Why did the universe bring this messy woman to me?

'So...' I start with nothing else to do but try to make her talk. 'The position?'

'Erm, yes.' She cranes a neck over her shoulder, looking back into the house as if she needs permission to talk to me. When she turns back to face me, her eyes lock with mine, and I no longer see fear – just pleading. 'Would you like to come in and talk about it?'

A beaming smile reaches my lips because now I'm seeing progress. Despite how cold the reception was – just like the bitter temperature outside – at least I now have an invite to speak with this woman and be considered for a role that will keep me busy.

Before stepping inside, I turn back to the taxi driver and give him a thumbs up. He doesn't return it. All he does is shake his head, start up the engine, and begin his perilous journey back down the hill. I didn't really want him to leave because I don't know how long I'll be in this house for. It could be five minutes or five hours.

Regardless, I go inside to marvel at the rest of the house.

I'm immediately taken aback by a grand staircase that rises up a massive hall and splits in two different directions. It reminds me of the one in the *Titanic* film, where Jack and Rose met more than once, both before and after the disaster. Hopefully, my luck will be better.

'Forgive me for being so rude at the door,' the woman says. 'We're not used to company up here. My husband hates random interruptions, which is why he chose to move us up here in the first place. But where are my manners? I'm Nora.'

'Emma,' I tell her, realising I already told her my name. 'You lived in town before?'

'Yes. Well, not for very long. We moved from Yorkshire and stayed in rented accommodation when we first moved here. This was long before we were blessed with Jacob. He's such a sweet boy, but he has trouble connecting with people.'

It doesn't surprise me. If I were locked up on a hill, I wouldn't be great with people either. Especially if that was the case from the day I was born. My own experience was far different – my parents always encouraged us to go out and socialise, although my social skills became much worse during my adolescence, favouring textbooks over nights out at university. Maybe that's why I'm so good with kids. I can still see my young, sociable self in them.

'Would you like a tour of the house?' Nora asks.

'Yes, please. If it's not too much trouble.'

I'm led down a wide hallway with multiple

doors on either side. There's a window at the end, but not much light gets in. We travel past the radiators, which are a blessed relief from the cold outside as heat seeps from the steel. Nora doesn't open any of the doors, probably just to maintain an ounce of privacy from this stranger who appeared on her doorstep. In fact, she doesn't guide me at all or so much as talk until we reach a kitchen that's bigger than the whole downstairs of the house I grew up in. I can practically hear my jaw hit the floor.

'Are you all right?' Nora asks in the perfectly posh voice that speaks money.

'Me? I'm fine. It's just that you have a magnificent home.'

'Thank you.' Nora smiles softly, which takes five years off her face. 'May I ask about your teaching experience? Judging from the suitcase you left by the door, I'm assuming you're new in town. Am I also to assume you haven't brought any previous employment details?'

'Well, yes. See, I'm something of a drifter. I like to take jobs wherever I can, hopping from place to place and seeing where my luck takes me. This time, it was Wedchester, but I had no idea it would be so hard to find work.'

'It's even harder if you didn't bring details of your employment history.'

'Touché. But I was honestly expecting to just work in a shop or warehouse or something.'

'So then, what brought you to my house?'

I'm trying to think of a better answer than 'there was nothing else available', and I stutter in my lead-up to excusing my laziness. 'Working in a sector I'm familiar with, in a beautiful house in a lovely town, meeting a wonderful woman who cares very much for her child's education... it's a hard thing to say no to.'

Nora examines me again, a small smile creeping onto one corner of her mouth. It's not like she doesn't see right through my charm, but she's amused by it at the very least. 'Well, in the interest of returning the flattery, I'm inclined to tell you I have a good feeling about you.'

After smiling back, we continue through the grand house, finding rich mahogany and oak everywhere there isn't marble. I tell her of the years I spent as a teaching assistant, helping the younger kids learn the alphabet while spending my evenings studying to become a full-time secondary school teacher. I detail the years I spent working in London, teaching English literature to thirteen-

and fourteen-year-olds. Nora tells me she expects more than just English, to which I inform her I'm qualified for much, much more. I'll provide references, of course.

Nora seems to approve, humming as she nods and continues our tour through the estate. I continue to be amazed by the size of the house. I stopped counting rooms after we passed the fifteenth, unable to help but notice that she ignored the one at the end of the hall.

I wonder what's in there.

We stop again in a large room that's somewhere between a library and a study. Nora looks around as if she's searching for something, all of a sudden ignoring my very presence. Is it that she wants to find someone in here, or – keeping in tone of the scared little squirrel vibe she's been giving me this whole time – does she want to make sure someone *isn't* here?

'Can I help you look for something?' I ask.

'No.' Nora returns to me. 'I'm looking for Jacob. He must be in his room.'

'How old is he?'

'Six. Would you like to meet him?'

I nod, and then she takes me up the *Titanic* stairs and down yet another hall. We stop at an open door, where clicking and clacking echoes from. Nora puts a hand on my arm, stops as if she wants to ask me something, then shakes her head and tries a different approach.

'He's not very good at communicating, so don't take it personally if he dislikes you.'

It doesn't worry me. I've met many kids who aren't fluent in making friends, and I've always found a way to get through to them. *Always*. I've worked in slums, rich areas, and everything in between. I'm pretty confident I can handle the son of a rich, happily married couple who live in what seems like complete isolation.

Speaking of which, where is Nora's husband?

I'm about to ask, but then she takes me into the room. It's a sickly vibrant bedroom with a Marvel duvet and so many bright colours it looks like something from a cartoon. A young boy of six is sitting at a small table, colouring perfectly between the lines of a *Toy Story* image, where Woody and Buzz are soaring through the air.

'Jacob,' Nora says from the doorway. 'I'd like you to meet Emma.'

Jacob doesn't move. He continues to colour without sparing me so much as a one-second glance. Nora looks at me and shrugs, then hugs her own chest as if she no longer knows what to do. I've met parents like her before – weak ones – and one thing is common among them.

They need all the help they can get.

'May I?' I ask, gesturing towards her son.

'Please.'

Carefully, I approach Jacob and kneel at his side. So as not to scare him with an overwhelming amount of attention, I keep my eyes on his drawing rather than him. '*Toy Story* was one of my favourite films when I was growing up,' I tell him with a fraction of honesty. 'I never did like the second one though. Do you?'

Jacob hasn't stopped colouring, but at least he shakes his head.

'You're really good at colouring. Can you show me how to stay within the lines?'

I feel slightly stupid, talking to him like he's three, but it seems to be working. The faintest smile creeps onto his lips as he pulls out another preprinted picture, this one of the same characters riding on the back of a remote-controlled car. Before I even get a chance to ask, he puts a pot of colouring pencils in front of me and leans in close as if to teach me.

It only takes one look at Nora to know what

she's thinking. It's in her smile, her posture speaking of relief as she sees her son open up just a little bit. I've seen that look before on many occasions, each time meaning the same thing.

I've got the job.

THAT'S AS FAR as I get with Jacob, colouring with him for a few minutes without another word between us. It sounds like a fail, but building that companionship and trust is vital to our relationship as a tutor and student. I say goodbye and leave the room in search of Nora, who left a few minutes ago with a big grin on her face.

I find her on the upstairs landing, the house deadly silent save for the tick-tock of the obnoxiously loud grandfather clock sitting dead in the centre. Nora is leaning against the banister and staring down into space, like a troubled queen observing her kingdom. There's worry in her drooping frown, which creates an air of sadness.

'Everything seems okay in there,' I tell her. 'Jacob is a lovely boy.'

'Yes, he is.' Nora perks right up but doesn't look at me. 'I think you'll fit right in here.'

'Thank you. I certainly hope so.'

The Private Tutor

'When are you able to start?'

'As soon as possible. I have no plans.'

'How about tomorrow morning?'

I nod and thank her as she escorts me down the stairs. There's still the matter of payment and finding a suitable place to live though. Temporarily, of course. To be honest, I'm in half a mind to ask about staying here, shacking up with the big, happy family in their enormous house. I just don't want to impose, but I'm surprised Nora doesn't offer. Sorry if that seems entitled.

Anyway, I'm more interested in the room at the end of the hall.

'Is something wrong?' Nora asks, following my gaze like she's reading my thoughts.

'Nothing at all. I just wondered what's in that room, but it's none of my business.'

'You're curious, and that's okay.' Nora smiles again. 'That's where my husband works. Richard is a very private man who likes keeping to himself. I'd very much like you to meet him, but he's working hard and doesn't like to be disturbed.'

'It's okay. What does he do?'

'He's a doctor. Though as you can imagine, it's hard to stay busy in a town this size. That's why he works from home, consulting via online video chats. It was a hard transition for him, but he seems happy with this new direction.'

I nod, not knowing what to say until it hits me. 'Well, I look forward to meeting him.'

Nora nods right back, then speedily opens the door. We say goodbye like old friends, all smiles as she buries her sadness behind it. There's something about Nora – a secret untold, like she has some great pain she's dying to share but just can't. I want to help her as well as her son, but I must learn not to cross those boundaries.

No good can come of it.

Chapter Three

Nora was at least kind enough to call me a taxi back into town. Thankfully, it's a different driver from last time, which saves me from a scowl and a bit of a headache. Not that it makes the journey any more bearable – the tyres lose their grip every five seconds, speeding us down the road faster and more aggressively than I can bear. All I can do to keep myself from soiling my pants is hold on for dear life and pray to survive the trip.

'Don't worry, love,' says the driver. 'I've done this many times.'

It's a little reassuring but not enough to make me unclench.

When we get to the high street, I pay the driver

a decent tip for getting me there in one piece, then ask where the best place to find some accommodation might be. He tells me there's a bed and breakfast just five minutes from here, then kindly offers to drop me up there for free as he's going that way anyway. I'm not too proud to take the free ride.

The house he leaves me at is a beautiful cottage with cobblestone walls and a garden full of dead grass. Given how well maintained everything else is, I put it down to winter killing the flowers, decide it's going to be a clean and well-kept house on the inside, then knock on the door. The driver leaves because if there's no space for me to spend the night here, I'll have to find the quietest bench in town and set up camp.

As luck would have it, a kindly, portly lady opens the door and greets me with a smile. She tells me her name is Martha, that she has a spare bed and can offer breakfast every morning along with dinner if I want it. I hesitate to accept until I've seen the room, which she quickly leads me up to and tells me the rate. It's affordable, but the room leaves much to be desired.

The first thing I notice is the smell – a mixture of mould and bleach. That immediately tells me this place is usually filthy, cleaned only during less busy times of year to attract more tourists. It shows, too – the wallpaper is stained yellow with smoke, some of it peeling and hanging from the wall in thin strips desperate to break free. Before the owner of this establishment can sell me on anything, I sit on the bed and sink with the creaky, rusty springs that squeak under my weight. I won't lie – it's agony.

'How long will you be staying?' she asks as if I've already accepted.

'Not sure at the moment. Can I pay for a month and go from there?'

She tries to hide her smile but fails. 'We can make that work, yeah.'

There are no papers to sign. It's a case of a simple card transaction and the handing over of a key, just like the good old days. Before I know it, I'm sitting alone in this bed with nothing but a suitcase to unpack and a plan to make for Jacob. I really hope I can do right by him.

As far as I'm concerned, failure is not an option.

. . .

After a horrible night's sleep and an undercooked breakfast, I make my way back up the hill on foot, leaving just as the sun rises to make sure I get there on time. There's even more slipping and sliding on ice to make me regret not taking a taxi. I don't care how much it would have cost – it would have been the lesser of two evils.

It's Nora who lets me in when I arrive, and she's just as pleasant as she was yesterday. She shows me to Jacob's room and asks if I need anything. I tell her no and ask if she's okay with me using my own schedule. She is, and it's nice to know she trusts me entirely.

When she leaves me alone, I head into the room.

'Morning, Jacob,' I say as I head through the open door and find him sitting back at the grotesquely bright red table. This time, there is no colouring book – just a Roald Dahl story he's got his face buried in, saying nothing at my merry greeting. I can tell this is going to be hard work. 'I've not read that one yet. Is it good?'

Jacob shakes his head. I drop the satchel off my shoulder and dump it onto the table, kneeling at his side and making sure he's paying attention. I know how important it is to make him engage me, so I point at the cover of his book and ask if he likes the illustrations.

All he does is nod.

Holding back a sigh, I open my bag and pull out a couple of textbooks, along with an unused notebook I tend to always keep two spares of. It's a habit that comes from my own time in school, where my drink bottle leaked all the time. It's nice to be prepared.

'Right, then,' I say, spreading the books apart in front of him. I have to stop myself from smiling when he sets aside his story and looks down at the options on the table. 'We're going to be splitting each of these subjects by morning and afternoon, setting aside one hour for creative play. That means drawing, colouring, or making things. I thought it might be nice for you to choose which lesson we start with. What do you say?'

Surprise, surprise, Jacob doesn't say anything. At least not until I suggestively tap on the English one as he's already made his interest in literature vaguely apparent. Like a shy little mouse creeping out of its hole for a chunk of cheese, he reaches forward to look at the textbook. The front cover shows a cartoon pirate aboard an impressive vessel, a high castle sitting in the background. It was specifically designed to attract younger readers.

I should know because an old friend of mine published it.

'This one,' he says at last, and it's great to hear his gentle little voice.

'That's a good choice,' I tell him, shoving the others aside. 'Do you like reading?'

'Yep.'

'Then you'll love today's studying. We're looking at *The Chronicles of Narnia*.'

There's not much for the kid to say, but that's all right. Most of it is me lecturing him as we read certain sections of *The Lion, The Witch, and the Wardrobe*, then stopping to ask him questions about the story. By eleven o'clock, we're at the section where Lucy has tea with Mr. Tumnus, and then we have to stop for the creative play. For this morning, Jacob wants to try a little fiction writing. Despite how little he's talking, I already feel like I've achieved something.

Lunchtime soon comes around. Nora knocks shyly on the door and tells Jacob to run down to the kitchen to grab the food she's laid out for him. He bolts for the door without further encouragement, leaving me alone in the room with my employer.

'How's it going?' she asks.

'Pretty well, I think.' Tidying up, ready for when we continue, I pack away the used textbook and get ready for a couple of hours of beginner mathematics. 'It didn't take long for him to show an interest – he's already enjoying being creative – but my main concern is that it's pretty hard to get a word out of him.'

'That will change,' she assures me. 'In time.'

I believe her. Most kids warm up after a while. It just takes a certain amount of interest in the subject being taught and a bond to form between the two of us. It will be okay, I tell myself, before my attention is stolen by Nora wringing her hands and hanging her head low.

'Are you okay?' I ask.

'Yes.' Nora nods, her hanging hair covering her painfully gaunt face.

'Are you sure? If there's something you need to talk about...'

She shakes her head, still hiding her face. I wonder what she's hiding – what harsh, painful secret she's keeping from me. It's not really any of my business, but when someone is in need, I feel an irresistible obligation to help them. But I suppose, just like her son, opening up to me will come in time. For now, I'll just assume it's how it looks.

That she's uncomfortable in her own home.

'Why don't you go and eat something?' she says, finally looking up at me with an excessively fake smile. 'I've prepared you a little something and left it in the kitchen.'

'Oh, you really shouldn't have.' Although I did forget to pack a lunch.

'It's no trouble. We have the money, and I have the time. All I ask is that you eat it away from Jacob. I want to make sure he gets the break he needs in the middle of such a tiring day.'

I agree and thank her, fully understanding and accepting her request. It works well for me, actually – I can have a few minutes to think, preparing myself for the rest of the day and figuring out how to encourage a relationship with Jacob. That's the best I can do.

Eat, then get straight back on the horse.

THE AFTERNOON GOES AS WELL as the morning… to start with anyway.

The Private Tutor

Mathematics was a bore for the pair of us – it never was my favourite subject – but we soon got around to the creative portion of the afternoon. I'm trying to insinuate that it's more of a reward than a part of the work itself, which seems to be having a positive effect as evidenced by his creative scribble across a previously blank A4 page.

While he continues to cover it with an explosion of colour, I sketch a little in my own book. Drawing always came easy to me. It's one of those things I don't have to think about, much like breathing. Once a pencil is in my hand, my subconscious does the rest. Perhaps that's why I quickly find myself with a drawing of my family – my sister and our parents standing in the doorway of a small London flat. We never were a very strong family, and that became even more true when Mum and Dad split. They went their separate ways, and it never got repaired.

I sigh with sadness and close the book, then sneak a peek at my watch. There are only thirty minutes left to go for today, and I'm starting to get a little sleepy. Stifling my yawn, I rub away the tear it produces, then peer down at Jacob's drawing, which is now so colourful that I can't make out the image. It's like a unicorn farted on the page.

'What are you drawing?' I ask, hoping not to suggest it's a bad piece of work.

'Katie,' he says shyly, adding yet more colour.

'Who's Katie?'

'My old tutor.'

The old woman from the café is in my head all over again, her words ringing through me like an alarm. *'Their last tutor... left town.'* I'd be lying if I said it didn't arouse some curiosity, but I'm not about to interrogate a young boy. Instead, I lean over to examine the drawing and see if it offers any clues as to what it is. I find nothing.

'What's this?' I ask, pointing to a long, brown shape with splashes of black in the middle.

'A dirt path.'

'And this?' My finger taps a grey structure.

'The well. It's in our garden.'

'Oh, I see it now.' Finally, I point to another grey shape. This one is darker, rectangular, and leaning over so far it might as well be sideways. 'And this thing right here?'

Jacob stops colouring, his eyes drifting over to where my finger is. 'That's Katie.'

Something about it doesn't seem right. Kids are notoriously bad at drawing – even the good ones – but there's no way in hell a human being can be confused with a blank, grey shape. When I ask him why it looks like that, the casualness with which he replies is enough to rip a chill right through me with an icy hand.

'Actually, Katie is underneath it,' he says. 'This is her grave.'

Chapter Four

It's not until the next day that I summon the courage to ask Nora about the grave.

A small part of me considered packing my bag and leaving town, driven from the town by fear of what I'd find out. But alas, I'm a grown woman with a rational mind, and the best thing for me to do is ask. I mean, what if Jacob just has an active imagination? What if he simply misunderstood what really happened to my predecessor?

Bright and early, I leave Jacob with a textbook to copy from and then head downstairs looking for Nora. I find her on the back patio, smoke drifting from the cigarette between her fingers as she stares out into the woods. The trees are tall and magnificently dense, even with the bare skeletons of their winter branches. There aren't many people lucky enough to have woods backing into their gigantic garden. This sure is one lucky family.

'Nora,' I say softly, trying not to startle her as I step out onto the patio.

She turns, looks me up and down like it's the first time she's ever seen me, then drops the cigarette into an empty coffee jar and tucks it behind a garden bench. 'Emma. What are you doing out here? Where's Jacob?'

'I left him with some work for a few minutes. He's okay. Can we talk?'

'Erm... okay. Is something wrong?'

While the whistle of the icy wind creeps between us, I'm trying to think of a good way to frame this question. There isn't one. 'Jacob drew a picture of a grave yesterday. He said his previous tutor was buried underneath it.'

Nora nods slowly, wrapping her arms around her chest as she shivers. After a long, exasperated sigh, she meets my eye. 'Little children and their fantasies, I suppose. We did have a tutor before you. Her name was Katie, and she was lovely, but Richard didn't like her much.'

'Why not?'

'Let's just say he has high standards.'

'It takes a lot to please him?'

'It's more than that. He's—'

'Right here,' booms a voice from behind me.

I spin around to face a tall, well-built man with a strong jaw and a five o'clock shadow beneath sandy hair and deep-set hazel eyes. I can't help noticing the way Nora takes a step back, her eyes widening as she spots her husband in the doorway.

What kind of woman is scared of her own husband?

'You must be Emily,' he says, locking his firm gaze on me.

'Emma,' I correct, stepping forward to shake his hand.

He takes it, albeit with reluctance. 'I trust Nora is treating you well?'

'Very well, yes.'

'And Jacob?'

'Everything is fine with your son. He's a good kid.'

'Yes, he is.'

Silence falls upon the patio. Richard is looking right through me, staring daggers at his wife as if she's caused him some kind of great upset. I wonder what's going on between them – what could possibly have caused such great distance to tear between them. Then I remember Katie, wondering just how much of a problem she was for them.

'I'd better get back to work,' Richard says. 'Just thought I'd introduce myself.'

'It's a pleasure to meet you. Thanks for the opportunity.'

Once again, he looks over me at Nora. 'Did you tell her about the phones?'

'No,' Nora says. 'Emma, we have a no-phone policy in this house.'

'You do? How come?'

'We simply don't want Jacob growing up with those things being commonplace.'

'How do you get any work done?' I ask Richard.

'Online, but it's not wireless. The only connection is in my office.'

No phone, no internet. Great. I try not to sound upset.

'Fair enough. I don't have a phone anyway.'

Silence comes again, this time with Richard watching me. It's like he's trying to see if I'm lying, which I'm not. I hate phones as much as the next person, and if I ever truly need one, I'll simply buy one. Although with how things are going up here –

with the fear Jacob's drawing instilled in me – it might be a good idea to do so.

Even if it does mean breaking their rule.

Richard lingers for a little longer before leaving us out in the cold. From the way Nora hid that cigarette so quickly, I'm starting to suspect she's not supposed to be doing it. Is there a controlling relationship between the two of them, with Richard being the authority? It wouldn't surprise me – his presence is still very striking even after he's gone.

'Well then, how about a cup of tea before returning to your duties?' Nora asks.

'Tea would be nice, thank you. Would it be okay if I took it upstairs with me?'

'I don't see why not.'

We head into the kitchen, where I'm once again blown away by its size. The Aga oven, the stunning blue tile, and the massive island in the middle of the room tell me this family has more money than God. If I were that rich, I wouldn't still be working as a doctor, but I understand some people aren't happy unless they're working.

The kettle bubbles as Nora sets about putting together two cups of tea. Sneakily, I poke my head outside the room to make sure we're not being listened to, then do my best to resume the conversation that brought me down here in the first place.

'So, about Katie…'

Nora pours boiled water into the mugs and then presses down the teabags. 'She was a lovely lady. Like you, only slightly younger. Had a very positive attitude and liked to get things done. You two would have got on really well.'

It's a nice thing to hear. I smile politely.

'The truth is, it's really not a good idea to start talking about what happened to her. It's too easy for things to be taken out of context, have words twisted, and that's how bad rumours start. As if those aren't bad enough already.'

'There's talk of her in town,' I say, regretting it instantly.

Nora slides a cup of tea towards me, her eyes opening wide. 'There is?'

'Not much, but a little. It seems like the big town secret.'

'That's what people are like. It's disappointing. What else do they say?'

'Only that you're a lovely family, which I'm inclined to agree with.'

'That's very kind.' Nora smiles and heaves a

sigh. 'Well, I suppose you'd better get back to your job. If there's anything you need, just search the house. I'll be around here somewhere. Catching up on some cleaning, most likely.'

I smile again, reach for my tea, then stop when I see it.

It's barely visible under her long sleeve, but when she makes the mistake of reaching for her mug, her sleeve recedes and reveals a dark purple bruise. I've seen a lot of bruises during my years as a teacher – caught a lot of bullies that way – and in spite of Nora being roughly the same age as me, my maternal instincts take over.

'What's this?' I ask, gently reaching out for her arm.

Nora withdraws. 'It's nothing.'

'It's not *nothing*. It's as purple as Vimto.'

'This doesn't concern you.'

'I'm just one woman looking out for another. Let me see.'

With a great deal of hesitation, Nora finally rolls up her sleeve ever so slowly, not daring to look at me. It doesn't come as a great surprise. A lot of abuse victims are embarrassed or ashamed about the way they're treated. There's no reason she should be any different.

I hold her hand with utmost care, examining her bare wrist. The bruise is like a spill of purple and yellow ink, oozing together in a way that's horrifically beautiful. I try not to wince, knowing it would take a great deal of pressure or a severely aggressive strike to cause such a mark. I touch it gently, and Nora winces, then rips it away from me.

'Who did this to you?' I ask, already having some idea of the answer.

'It's not... If I... Can we just leave it be?'

'Not really.'

'Please, Emma. You don't understand.'

I watch her with great sympathy, studying the way she avoids looking into my eyes and hurries to hide her arm from further examination. It's not uncommon for victims of domestic abuse to want to keep it to themselves, but she is ultimately right.

It doesn't concern me.

Nora leaves with her cup of tea, saying no more on the matter. I'm tempted to press, but upsetting either one of my employers is not a good idea. The best I can do is keep my head down and continue to perform the job I'm being paid to do. Though it won't hurt to keep an eye on Nora, as long as I do it discreetly.

I don't want to get her into trouble.

When I return to Jacob, it's hard to get much more out of him than a yes or a no. I'm trying my best to teach him about gravity and its effects on our big, blue planet. It's hard to tell if he's interested – his freckled little face is cupped in both hands as he watches the book I refer to, but he doesn't even bother to brush aside the sweep of chestnut hair. It's like he's bored but is too polite to complain about having to sit through this.

After what I just learned about Nora, I can't stop thinking about Richard. I have already got a sense of the kind of man he was – authoritative and stern – but seeing the bruise on his wife's arm tells me everything I need to know and more.

I've got to steer clear of him where possible.

As soon as we're done with the lesson on gravity, Jacob asks me if it's okay to swap creative time with reading some more of his Roald Dahl book. He's been extremely well behaved and is learning at a speed I didn't even think was possible, so I tell him it would be fine as long as he stops after thirty minutes (just so I can give him a quick maths test). He doesn't waste any time in running to his bedside table and grabbing the book, then throwing himself onto the mattress to see how his current story plays out. It's funny, I barely know the kid, but I'm so proud of his insatiable hunger for literature.

Anyway, for as long as he's distracted by a book, I have a few spare minutes to run to the bathroom and 'squeeze the lemon', as my mother used to so proudly phrase it. Of all the people in my estranged family, she's probably the one I miss the least.

Only I don't make it to the bathroom.

Out in the hall, just when I think I'm alone, the voices echo through the hall and travel down the corridor. It's like a funnel for their voices, amplifying their every syllable. I shouldn't be nosy – it's not my business, so I should just carry on and... well, do my business – but with the content of their conversation, it's hard to overlook.

So I stop, and I listen.

'For the last time, I don't want you explaining the situation to the help,' Richard's voice angrily rings up through the hall. 'What happened to Katie is between you and me. If you're having trouble understanding that, then we're in some serious trouble.'

Nora speaks with a half sob. 'I'm sorry. She asked me out of the blue, and—'

'Enough of the excuses, for crying out loud. And what about the bruise?'

'What about it?'

'Did you tell her the truth about where it came from?'

'No. I mean... of course I didn't, no.'

'Then what *did* you tell her?'

The conversation goes quiet then. It's unclear whether they're still talking or if there's just a pause in the middle, but the temptation to listen in has grown far too great. I tiptoe down the hall, wary of the groaning floorboards that quietly announce my presence. If this squabble turns into something more, I want to be there for Nora. To protect her, I guess.

As if one thirty-six-year-old skinny blonde can save another.

I creep a little close to the main hall, where the conversation has still gone dead. That's where I freeze at the sound of footsteps, trying to figure out if they're coming closer or moving further away. But when Richard calls out, the question answers itself.

'Is someone up there?' he yells. 'Jacob? Emily?'

Emma, I think while looking back at the bathroom door.

Before I can get caught eavesdropping, I scurry back up the hall and disappear into the bathroom. The footsteps outside grow louder, but I don't think anyone saw me coming in. As far as they're concerned, I could have been in here for a while and not heard a word they said. It'll be safer if I stay in here for a while to avoid confrontation, but during this time, I stay perched on the edge of the bath and wait a few minutes, thinking.

I really do have to ask myself the question.

Why am I so afraid of that man?

Chapter Five

It feels too early to deserve a day off, but I'm told not to work weekends. My younger self would be over the moon to hear such news, but now I'm faced with the trouble of what to do with myself. I don't care for walking out in the cold, and there doesn't seem to be much to do around Wedchester. It briefly crosses my mind that I could abandon my duties and find a new town – somewhere with a bit of life – but I feel a duty towards Jacob.

Besides, his mother put her trust in me.

I want to honour that.

The best idea I have is to head to one of the charity shops on the high street and pick out a book or two. I'm not a fussy reader, so I quickly select a couple of James Patterson novels, pay more than the asking price (anything for a kids' charity), then take them to the nearest pub, where I can settle in with some food and a glass or two of wine. It's not something I can spend the whole day doing, but it'll pass a couple of hours.

The pub is surprisingly quiet, with just a couple of people I assume are locals hanging out at the bar. The food is mediocre, which is to be expected of pub chips and a steak and ale pie. But it hits the spot, and hot food on a cold day is one of the finer things in life. As I've been told multiple times throughout my life, I'm pretty easy to please. With that being true, it's a wonder I don't have a boyfriend.

Just as that thought passes through my head, I start to ruminate about my past loves. They've all been pretty good men, just incompatible with someone like me. My style has always been to move around as often as possible, only sticking around in one town long enough to give the children's education a head start. I wish I knew what's wrong with me – what genetic malfunction has kept me from being able to settle. But we'll never truly know.

A few pages into my book, the pub door opens. Two ladies walk in, both in their forties, with tattered leopard-skin coats and highlights that grew out months ago. Their voices are loud and shrill, both cackling like witches, while one of them makes a beeline for the bar to order some drinks. The other stands in the doorway.

Her hard stare fixed on me.

'Oi, you're that teacher, aren't you?' she calls.

I take a quick glance around to double-check she's talking to me, then give her a short nod. She nods back, but I bury my nose back in my book. I don't know the human condition as a whole, but it's pretty likely she wants to cause some sort of trouble. I'm not good at arguing, much less at fighting, so I try keeping to myself.

That lasts all of five seconds.

The woman approaches me, pulling out a seat as her friend asks what she's drinking. 'Guinness,' she calls back, then puts a hand on my book and lowers it. My heart is racing as she grins, her eyes boring into me. 'Yeah, you took that job, didn't you? On the hill?'

'Yes,' I say weakly, praying nothing bad comes of this.

'Well, you'd better be careful. It ain't exactly the safest place on Earth.'

I can't tell if she's friendly or not, but that last

comment has my curiosity. I close my book and lean forward, my mouth hanging open while I try to figure her out. 'Why do I get such a bad feeling about that house? What happened?'

'You don't know?'

I shrug.

'I suppose you ain't the only one in the dark. To tell the truth, we've all been wondering what really went on up there. All we know for sure is that the last teacher – oi, what was her name?' she calls back to her friend.

'Kayleigh or Katie,' her friend offers from afar.

'That's it.' The woman snaps her fingers. 'Katie. She worked up there for a year or so. Always complained things were getting too much. Said she had a weird relationship with the man of the house, but none of us knew what she meant.'

I reach for my wine and take a long sip, which turns into an even longer draw. It's not because I'm thirsty, but this story is doing things to my body I can't explain. Is this intrigue or nervousness I'm experiencing right now?

'Anyway, she went up there one day and never returned. Some people say they saw her leaving town, but they could just be looking for attention, you know? Like, "look at me because I know things you don't". Thing is, the police went up there to look for her.'

I suddenly think of the grave drawing. 'Right. What did they find?'

'Nothing. Nobody got arrested either, and it's still a mystery.'

The woman's friend returns with a couple of pints. She berates her friend for bothering me, and then they each go outside to smoke in the beer garden. I'm left alone with nothing to do but worry about what went wrong in that house, what might happen to Richard's family if he's left alone with them, and then wonder – selfishly – what will happen to me?

I SPEND the whole of the next day in my room at the bed and breakfast. It's not because I'm unsociable, but the extreme weather warnings are starting to scare me. The winds outside are bad to look at even from a cosy (smelly) rented room, but when you step outside and realise just how cold those winds are, you'd be dumb as a bag of rocks to go for a wander.

Besides, I can't stop thinking about the woman in the pub. Since she mentioned that the police had investigated Katie's disappearance, it's brought a certain amount of reality to the situation. As if it's more than just speculation but is, in fact, a formal legal enquiry. I should be too scared to go back up to that house – and believe me, I've thought about running – but the fact the police didn't arrest Richard or Nora tells me it's probably safe.

At least, that's what I'm telling myself.

Sadly, it's not like I can take to the internet for answers. Martha, my landlady, informs me she'll never have the internet in her home because strangers could easily look up illegal stuff and blame it on her. I don't know enough about the inner workings of the web to tell her she's wrong, but it's still a disappointment. Nothing would please me more than to spend my Sunday devouring every article I could find about the private tutor that came before me.

But it does give me a chance to unwind, to some degree. With the gales blasting past the window, forcing the trees to lean towards the ground as the gate outside rocks within the confines of the bolt that secures it, I get to sit by my window and read more of the James Patterson book I started yesterday. Not that I can concentrate very much – my mind keeps going back to Katie, and I wonder if I'll share a similar fate.

I'd be silly not to reconsider leaving town. There's nothing for me here except misery and a misplaced sense of loyalty to Nora and Jacob. Sure, they've survived this long without me, but what if something happens? What if Richard finally snaps and goes all Jack Torrance on his family? I could be the one who stopped that from happening, even if just by being there.

It's starting to hurt my head.

I close the book and sigh, then stare out the window at the weather. It's getting dark out there, and I can just about discern the lights glowing from atop the hill. The house is alive, but no matter how hard I try to tell myself otherwise, I can't help thinking Katie isn't.

Come Monday, I've already made up my mind.

I'm going to stay.

At least for the time being. There's no telling how bad things are going to get when I'm caught in the middle of a potentially abusive marriage, and then there's the weather that's threatening to blow us all inside out. To be completely honest, I'm starting to regret coming to this town in the first place. I thought it was going to be easy.

It's anything but.

This particular morning starts off even worse. The temperature has dropped by a few more degrees, and the roads are caked in ice. Walking up to the house would be an absolute nightmare, but the taxi service informs me they won't be operating until some of the ice starts to thaw. I take a little glance up at the hill, the sun cresting over it as if to illuminate the road like a band of crystals. Which isn't technically accurate – at least crystals are alluring.

Unlike the hike up that hill is going to be.

Nonetheless, I have no choice. I promised Nora her son would get a good education from me, so I throw on my shoes with the best grip and embark up the hill using a tree branch as a trekking pole. There are multiple near fatalities even when I stick to the grass, but somehow, I make it to the very top. Even though my fingers are frozen in the tight grip that refuses to let go of the branch, I'm so glad to have made it here safely.

Nora lets me in just like the other mornings, except this time, she pulls me to one side prior to the lesson. It's important that I hear her out, she says, waving me into a room I've never been in before. This one has two red leather sofas and a few bookshelves lined with leather-bound tomes that I sincerely doubt anyone actually reads. There's so much dust on the small table beside the sofas that I'm not sure anyone ever comes in here. Judging from the dank gloominess of it, I wouldn't use it either. Not even if it were my house.

'I've been thinking about what you asked me,' Nora says. 'About my bruise.'

'Oh?'

'I'm not ready to tell you how it came to be, but would you do me a kindness?'

'Of course. What do you need?'

Nora looks over her shoulder, then, still frowning, takes a few extra steps to lean out of the door and make sure nobody is around. When she returns to me, she takes both my hands and looks me dead in the eye. 'It's really good to have you here. Not just so Jacob has a consistent tutor, but when you're here, Richard doesn't... I mean, he's...'

'Take your time,' I say soothingly.

'Yes. I shouldn't...' She clears her throat. 'I don't want you to leave. Not for a long time.'

I'm stunned, not quite sure of the best way to react. I don't intend to leave, but her begging me to stay here only goes to show how desperate this woman is. It will only take a few words to calm her. 'I'm not going anywhere. Is that the kindness you wanted from me?'

'Yes.' Nora watches me, nodding slowly. 'Please, promise me. No matter what—'

'S*now*!'

We both startle at the excited voice screaming from the nearby door. Nora lets out a little yelp of fear while I take a step back, proving once and for all how much of a coward I am. I'm relieved to see it's just Jacob, sprinting towards the window as if Christmas is going to come two months in a row. His little hands slap against the pane as he screams again that it's snowing – oh my God, it's actually snowing! – which terminates my conversation with Nora.

Not that it stops us. She continues begging with her eyes.

And with my own, I make that promise.

I'm not going to leave her up here.

Chapter Six

It's been a great start to the week, all things considered.

I haven't seen Richard a single time, and Nora has pretty much kept to herself. This gave me plenty of time to sit with Jacob and put some serious investment into his education. I still haven't broken down the walls that keep him from warming to me the way most kids do, but we're getting there – he's already willing to learn, not attempting to fight me when I tell him about the day's workload. Although we probably have my creative play idea to thank for that.

A whole day passed by without problems, and the snow is still coming down quite heavily by the time I leave. I half expect Nora (or at least Richard) to offer me a lift down the hill, but no such kindness arises. It's like they *want* me to slip and fall. I can almost picture Richard's stern face, his lips finally curving upwards into a smile as I tumble and break my leg.

Isn't a doctor supposed to do the exact opposite?

When I eventually make it back to my piece-of-crap rented room, I hurl myself onto the bed and fall asleep right away. My vivid dreams throw awful images at me, of Nora running to me all beat up, bruises covering her cheeks like face paint as she struggles to talk through her tears. Jacob is standing somewhere behind her, screaming, 'Mum! Mum!'

It takes a while for me to realise he's not calling Nora.

He's calling, 'Emma! Emma!'

I awake with misery clinging to my foggy brain. Shaking it off the best I can, I fill up on breakfast, stuff my laptop into my satchel (I still can't believe nobody around here has the internet), then begin yet another dangerous trip up the hill. By the time I get there, my cheeks are so numb they feel like concrete slabs hanging off my previously youthful face. How long now until I start to look my age?

Current stress levels accounted for, probably not long.

Nora lets me in, and I spend the whole morning with Jacob. He's such a nice kid; I just wish he would talk a little more. Not that I can blame him – he's been locked up on this hill for most of his life. Even if he made it into town, there isn't a whole lot he can do to keep himself occupied. But at least I can provide him with an education.

This class is interrupted, however, when a tall shadow stretches over me and creeps across the table we're sitting at. I turn and see Richard, only now sensing his musky cologne. It has a hot, overpowering smell, like smoking wood. It suits him – there's fire in his eyes.

'Emma,' he says snappishly. 'Can I see you out in the hall?'

At least he got my name right this time, I think as I nod and excuse myself from Jacob, leaving him with another textbook to copy from. Then, feeling like a naughty student who's about to receive some kind of punishment, I slink past Richard and stand in the hall.

That's when he closes the door and steps up close to me.

Too close.

Richard's breath is warm, a slight whiff of something unpleasant announcing itself as he speaks. 'I have a question,' he says, 'and the only thing I want from you is the honest truth. No lies, and no trying to spare my feelings. Is that understood?'

Suddenly, my mouth has gone dry. I peer over his shoulder to see if Nora might be there to rescue me – as if she's going to do a one-eighty and miraculously become the strong one in their relationship. Then I remind myself of the bruise on her wrist and know it's not going to happen. Not in this lifetime.

'Emma,' he snaps.

My body betrays me. I jump back, try to hide it, and fail. 'Yes, of course. What is it?'

'You've been living in town for a few days now, so what do they know?'

'What do they *know*?'

'Yes. What are they saying about us?'

If the goal is to not make him angry, the last thing I should tell him is the truth – that it's apparently not entirely safe up here because the tutor who came before me was never heard from again. But he did ask for the truth, so on the off-chance he already knows the answer and is simply testing my loyalty to his family, it would be a dumb idea to lie.

'Emma,' he says again, raising his voice to prompt me.

'Yeah. No. I don't know, really.' A casual shrug is what I'm aiming for, but my shoulders are so tense they never come back down. 'They seem to know a lot about Katie.'

Richard frowns. 'What exactly are they saying?'

'That she disappeared.'

'Is that it?'

'And there was a police enquiry.'

'It wasn't an enquiry.'

'It wasn't?'

'No. It was much more than that. They searched the whole premises.'

My mouth is so dry I can feel the texture of my teeth against my grainy tongue. A small ball of nerves lodges in my throat as I look into this man's hazel eyes and wonder just what he's capable of. Katie obviously did something to piss him off, so shouldn't I tread lightly?

It's so hard not to ask all the questions rattling around in my head.

'What about Nora?' he asks.

'What about her?'

'Are they talking about our marriage?'

'Not really,' I lie, and this one slips out simply because the truth is guaranteed to enrage him. I've heard a little talk around town – the odd comment on how Nora always seems afraid around her own husband or that she had a mark and blamed it on a loose paving stone. The same kind of excuses I've heard with my own ears, too.

Not that I'd tell him that.

'There's nothing else, I promise.'

'So that's it? They just mention Katie is gone?'

'Yep, that's it.'

'And what's the speculation?'

'About Katie?'

'Yes. They must have a theory?'

Of course they do, but I'm not about to tell him that. They all think he killed her, buried her somewhere she won't be found, then went home and carried on with his perfect, isolated little life. Honestly, I'm surprised they haven't come up here with pitchforks and flaming torches. For all the good it will do them – it won't bring Katie back.

'They just say you never got caught.'

'*Caught?*' Richard booms.

I shrink back again. 'You know, prosecuted.'

'So they think I killed her and got away with it?'

'No. Well, yes, but—'

'Next time they talk like that, I want you to put them straight. Understood?'

I nod, fighting back a stream of tears as I fear for my own safety. Richard's eyes are alive with ire, his size and obvious strength enough to intimidate and his deep, booming voice doing the rest of the work. I swallow a dry lump and continue nodding as he sizes me up.

'Good,' he says. 'That's a good response.'

As he finally turns and leaves, pounding up the corridor on the wooden floorboards so hard he causes an echo, I'm unable to move. It's been a long time since I've felt cold, numbing fear so deep that it's rooted me in place. Long after he's gone, I still stand there like an idiot thinking about my first encounter with Richard – my first *real* encounter – and wonder what might have happened if I'd argued with him. Would I have ended up injured like Nora or mysteriously vanishing like Katie? Either way, I have a terrible feeling.

I just narrowly escaped something awful.

. . .

The Private Tutor

When I finally stop myself from shaking, I return to Jacob's room and find him quickly scurrying away from the door. There's no use in him trying to pretend he wasn't just eavesdropping, so I don't blame him when he stops and turns to face me.

'Are you okay?' he asks.

'Yes, thank you,' I say formally, like I'm nothing more than his tutor. Then, when I stare into his eyes and see hints of his father, my eyes begin to water. I dab them with my sleeve and ask if he's had a cat up here, blaming it on my allergies.

'You don't need to pretend,' he says. 'I know he's scary.'

A six-year-old should not be looking at his father in that light, so I know something is majorly wrong with this family. I just hope that, whatever it is, it hasn't been transferred to Jacob by way of biological inheritance. It certainly doesn't look like it – there's a kindness in his eyes that makes me want to befriend him. A vulnerability that makes me want to scoop him up in my arms and tell him everything is going to be okay.

I wish someone would do that for me, too.

It's extremely difficult to do, but I sit him down and try to carry on with the lesson. It comes as no surprise that not a single word has been copied from the textbook. Jacob had his ear pressed against the door, and I don't blame him. Richard shouted so loud it could have woken someone from a coma, and it would take a great deal of restraint to not want to listen in. I'm just sorry he had to hear it, which is why I'm trying so hard to make him focus on the work rather than the monster his father is. If I'm honest, I'm trying to distract myself as well.

At least the rest of the day goes smoothly. Jacob tries his best, as usual, and I say goodbye while preparing for my venture back down the hill. It's not quite dark outside yet, but it's getting there, so I need to hurry. Nora does stop me, however, just as I'm nearing the door.

'Come back,' she says, stopping at my side.

'Sorry?'

'I heard Richard shouting at you. I'm so sorry he did that, but please don't let it scare you away from tutoring our son. He's doing really well with you, so please... come back tomorrow morning. I'll increase your pay if that's what it takes.'

As I stare into her eyes, I see nothing but fear. Insecurity. There's no way in hell I'm going to accept a pay rise just to do the right thing, so I promise I'll come back as many times as she needs. Although I do wish she'd offer me to stay up here. The trips up and down the hill are more than just excruciatingly exhausting.

They're insanely dangerous.

Nora smiles thinly and falsely, then stands in the doorway while I trudge back down the hill. I take my precious time, in no rush to beat the coming of night, even as the sun now sets on the horizon. The cold is bitter up here, and I don't want to get lost in it, but I'm not going to risk hurrying and slipping. So I take it one step at a time, my mind weighed down with thoughts of Richard and Jacob and the poor boy's mother. It's going to be years before I forget any of this. *If* I can ever forget it.

After about five minutes, an icy patch of frozen mud gives way under my foot. I stumble, spin as I fall, then catch myself on a gatepost. Struggling to maintain my balance, I lean against the post and take a final glance back at the house.

That's when I see Nora, still standing there.

She raises a hand, a single, motionless wave. I wave back with my gloved hand, sensing her worry that I won't return. The poor woman is frightened to death of being left alone with her husband, and there's no hiding it. It's in her every movement – her every terrified, mousy little word that leaves her trembling lips.

That's when it clicks.

This whole time, I wondered why she wasn't inviting me to stay in one of their many spacious rooms. At first, I thought it was because she wanted to keep her house private, maintaining some form of peace in their fortress of solitude.

I couldn't have been more wrong.

It's so obvious now in the way she keeps checking up on me. In how she refrains from talking about her husband and hides her bruises. She's not making me stay in town because of her – she's making me do it because of *me*. She's trying to keep me safe from the same danger she faces on a daily basis. The same danger Katie faced.

Right up until she disappeared.

Chapter Seven

THE SKY IS THREATENING snow again, and I'm hoping it won't settle. Even though I got back to my room safely, I sincerely hope this isn't it. Call me crazy, but I actually *want* to go back to that house, so I'm going to keep throwing caution to the wind and praying I don't get snowed in from either side. My ability to come and go is the only thing keeping me sane.

After dinner – a slow-cooked beef stew that's bursting with flavour but not too filling – I say an early goodnight to Martha and retire to my dismal room. It's there, lying on the bed and hopelessly unable to sleep, that I wish I had the internet. Nothing would please me more than to sit up for a couple of hours, researching the truth about what happened up there. That's when I realise there's a Wedchester encyclopaedia in the next room.

Her name is Martha.

Steeling myself to learn more than I should, I throw on a hoodie, debate changing out of my pyjama bottoms, then finally decide to just head to the communal room where – and this is no exaggeration – I have never seen a single soul.

Tonight is different because Martha is sitting there with a book, her apron off and her hair down. I've never seen her this relaxed, and it's nice. Despite how polite she is, she always appears so highly strung. It makes me feel bad for what I'm about to do.

'Sorry to interrupt,' I say from the doorway, 'but can I ask you something?'

Martha smiles, crow's feet appearing in the corners of her kind eyes as she closes a book and sits forward, setting it on the coffee table. 'Of course you can. Feel free to take a seat. Don't mind me – I'm just taking a few minutes off before bed.'

I smile and sit next to her, sinking into the old, torn, flower-patterned sofa that smells faintly of home-cooked meals. 'I've been working up at the house atop the hill, and there's been a lot of rumours about the tutor who went missing. I was wondering, since we don't have the internet, if you happen to know the outcome of the police investigation.'

The positivity leaves her eyes, her smile drooping into a frown. 'Yes, I can tell you what I know, but I'm afraid it's no more than anyone else does. It goes without saying that you should hand in your resignation as soon as possible.'

I know very little about this woman, but I get very genuine vibes off her. It's not like her advice is going to change my mind – not when I'm so invested in Nora and Jacob – but I want to hear what she has to say. Even if it does scare me silly.

'It was all over the papers,' she begins, clasping her hands around her protruding belly. '"Tutor Mysteriously Vanishes in Private Employment", it said, or something of the like. I actually met her. She was a delightful lady.'

'So she stayed here?' I piece together.

'Only for one night, but then she was offered a room under Richard's roof.'

'And she took it?'

'Aye. That was the last time I saw her, to be honest. I said that to the police, for as much as they wanted to listen. But I think they were overwhelmed with witness statements because other people claimed to have seen her. Don't ask me about none of that because I just don't know, but I remember the incident very well.

'It was only a year ago, but so much happened in a town where nothing else does. We all watched the police come and go up there, searching the entire property from top to bottom. It took them days – you've seen the size of the place – but they didn't find anything. All the hairs, fingerprints, and so on were to be expected. She worked there, after all, but it was Richard they were interested in more than anything else.'

I crane my neck to look at her, studying the sorrow in her expression. From the little I know about Martha, it's more than evident she has a heart. It probably keeps her more attached than she's comfortable with.

'Why Richard?' she asks.

'Well, rumour started to spread that he had a thing for Katie.'

'Like... romantically?'

'Romantically, sexually. However you want to phrase it. They were only rumours, so the police couldn't exactly arrest him based on the strength of that. But they *did* question him over and over. Not that it got them anywhere. Katie never showed up.'

It's hard to feel safe with a comment like that, but my sympathy for Nora far outweighs my good sense. Even if I tried to leave, I'd never be able to live with myself knowing I'd left them up there. Besides, the mystery surrounding my predecessor is far too alluring.

'To this day,' Martha says, 'the case remains unsolved. Some say she's still up there, hidden between the walls – that's how folklore starts, and you can blame the local kids for such nonsense – but I personally believe Katie was killed, taken away, and buried.'

Jacob's drawing flashes in my mind's eye. It causes a deep shudder that almost hurts.

'All I'm saying is you should be careful up there.' Martha pats my knee, then reaches for her book and fingers through the pages before falling back into the sofa. 'If I were you, I would stay in town. Far out of Richard's way.'

I know, I know. Going back up to that house after hearing all of that is one of the dumbest things a person could do. The thing is, I'm stubborn by nature. My mother was, my father was, and the apple doesn't fall too far from the tree.

It's anybody's guess what the weather is doing. Sleet starts, threatening snow. Snow comes during my hike up the hill, but it stops just as quickly. I try not to concern myself with the confusing workings of our weather cycle and just focus on seeing Jacob.

After all, I have a question for him.

One I really shouldn't be asking.

I wait until the afternoon, when he's woken up, enjoyed creative play and his lunch break, then returned to his room, where I wait for him with a chocolate treat and a new Roald Dahl book I picked up from one of the town's charity shops. It instantly puts him in a good mood, but I feel bad for attempting to buy his affections. It's technically exploitation.

Jacob takes the treat, thanks me, and wolfs it down with a big grin on his face. I sit back in the ridiculously uncomfortable beanbag chair, crossing my arms and watching him. Bless him – he deserves a treat after the crappy life he's had.

I just hope he doesn't tell his mother.

'Jacob, I need to ask you something, okay?'

Jacob stops eating, his lips dirtied with melted chocolate. He licks it off, then nods.

'A few days ago, you drew a picture of a grave. Do you remember that?'

'Yeah.'

'You said Katie was underneath it. Can you tell me why you said that?'

Jacob shakes his head and continues nibbling on the chocolate.

This is going to take more work. The kid might know something that's pivotal to figuring out the tutor's whereabouts. If there's anything I can do to help squeeze it out of him – anything at all – it would be mad not to try my best.

So I sit forward and continue.

'There has to be a reason, Jacob. You're not going to be in trouble for talking about it. Whatever you say to me stays in this room. Do you understand?' I place a hand on his shoulder. He recoils, and I pull away. 'This is our own private little conversation. I promise I won't tell anyone what you say. But I need to know about Katie.'

After a long, thoughtful pause, Jacob puts down his chocolate and stares at it. It's no longer the most important thing in his world, which worries me. When he opens his mouth to talk, that concern amplifies to a dizzying extent.

'Daddy has a temper,' he says.

'What makes you say that?'

'Mm.' He shrugs. 'Sometimes he hurts Mummy.'

'Did he ever hurt you?'

'Not yet?'

'*Yet?*'

'I think he would hurt me if I be naughty. So I try to be good.'

I know better than to press on that. It's bordering on childhood trauma, and I don't want to be responsible for causing a rift. Much less be punished by Richard when I'm caught for doing so. I sit there and choose my next question carefully.

'Is his temper why you think she's buried?' I ask.

'Yeah. Katie didn't like it here.'

'She didn't?'

Jacob nods, misery taking over his innocent little face. 'Can we do some work now?'

I suck in a deep breath and try to put this past me. It's just so hard to do. It's my duty – morally and professionally – to act on information like this. The problem is how to do it. I'll have to speak with Nora as soon as possible because this is too much of a bombshell to keep to myself. Anyway, I know what happens to abused women when their husbands get caught. I'll have to be discreet. Secretive.

Until then, we study.

Before leaving the house in the afternoon, I find Nora in the main hallway. Once more, she's so deep in her own thoughts that she doesn't notice me, only this time, she's sitting on the oak bench that faces the door. It looks like a church pew, and she seems to be silently praying. I can only imagine what it is she's asking the good Lord for.

Escape, probably.

'We need to talk,' I say, sitting beside her on the bench (pew).

Nora doesn't move a muscle – she simply sits dead-eyed, staring at the door as if I've been sitting here this whole time. 'Is there something I can help you with?'

'Yes, there is.' I take a deep breath. 'I need you to make a decision about something.'

'What might that be?'

'Your son tells me his father has a temper. I'm not going to lie – I've seen the bruise on your arm and the way he talks to you. I've overheard him shouting, and he even took time out of his busy day to raise his voice to me. Given what I know about Katie, it's hard not to put two and two together.'

Nora opens her mouth to talk, but I cut her off.

'You don't need to tell me. That secret is for you and the police. All I want to do is make sure that little boy upstairs is safe. And you, Nora, don't seem to have much of a handle on this. I'm really sorry if I'm overstepping, but if it's not safe up here, then we need to act.'

What happens next is beyond my expectation. A weird, choking sound comes from Nora's mouth. She cups her hands to her face, her shoulders bobbing up and down as she sobs into her palms. 'It wasn't supposed to be like this. Richard and I loved each other so much. He was my best friend. But after I got pregnant, he became more and more distant. It was like he despised me. The way he talked to me completely changed. The things he did...'

She turns to me, holds my hands in hers. I feel her warm tears on my fingers.

'Please don't involve the police,' she begs. 'You're right – something is wrong with my husband – but if you call the police, then he'll get even angrier. There's no telling what he'll do then. And with Katie...'

I wait, my breath caught in my throat as I linger on her next words.

'Please, Emma. Whatever you do, don't make things worse than they already are.'

'I won't tell them. Not without your permission. But this is something they can really help you with. Especially if you fear for your safety and even more so if you fear for Jacob's. They have protocols in place to protect people like you.'

'No.' Nora shakes her head and looks me right in the eye. Tears sparkle before rolling down her cheeks. 'I don't want anything to change. I love Richard, in spite of the things he does. Just give me a chance to see if things will iron out, all right? There's still hope for me and Richard. My best friend is still in there somewhere.'

God, I hope she's right. She's taking a gamble with her son's future in all of this. Not that I hold it against her – I've had an abusive boyfriend before, and the fear truly is paralysing. Maybe that's why I'm not rushing down the hill to contact the police.

Basically, I understand.

'Promise me, Emma,' she says. 'Promise me you'll give this a chance to resolve itself.'

'Okay, okay. I promise.'

'Thank you,' she says, weeping.

Even now, looking into her eyes, I know this is going to end badly. Men like Richard don't change. Nora and Jacob are in the firing line, just like I am. Just like Katie was. The worst part of it all is that nobody truly knows what happened to her. And if we ever find out?

Well, by then, it might be too late.

Chapter Eight

Each day is growing increasingly uncomfortable.

Today is no exception. I'm sitting with Jacob while he writes out his times tables, terrified that Richard is going to make another appearance. Nora is pottering around the house, taking to cleaning – and smoking where it's possible to get away with it – while I teach her son. Meanwhile, her husband is working in the isolation of his office again. I can't help but wonder if this is contributing to his aggression. I know how it works by now; frustration becomes solitude, solitude becomes boredom, and boredom leaves room for him to think about how unhappy he is with his living situation. It's only a matter of time until he blames that on Nora. Or worse than that – his own son.

I'm doing a similar thing myself. My eyes have been trained on the nearby window ever since Jacob started his test. The snow is coming down harder than ever now, slushing against the window and sliding down the glass. It settles on the windowsill, but unlike recent days, it doesn't melt away. I have a feeling it's going to stay this time, and my heel is automatically tapping against the carpet as I dreadfully anticipate getting snowed in.

I want to leave. That's not something I have trouble admitting to myself. But while Jacob is struggling with multiplying anything above six or seven, I can't leave him. I don't *want* to either. I promised I wouldn't leave this kid in the dark, and a promise means everything to me.

'What's five times nine?' Jacob asks, tearing me from my trance.

'Forty-five. Here, let me show you a trick.'

I rotate his book and write out a list, explaining that the answers for the nine times table decreases by one on the second digit. Then, I make him write it, amazed by how quickly he learned what I just taught him. It takes him less than a minute, scoring down the numbers as he mouths them: 'Fifty-

FOUR, sixty-THREE, seventy-TWO.' A smile works the corner of his mouth upwards, hopefully feeling the same sense of pride I am.

He's getting it, and he's getting it fast.

A gust of freezing air thrashes against the window, as if to hurl snow directly at us. The wind is howling, and it's getting worse. It's only a matter of time until I'm stuck up here, as if locked in a prison where there are no guards, no rules. And if the rumours about Katie's grim fate are anything to go by?

No escape.

It's time I ask Nora if I can leave early.

Who knows how this will go? It's evident she likes me being here, even if just so she gets a sense of security. I can't say I blame her either, but that doesn't give her a right to keep me here if it means I can't go home. It's already getting pretty bad out there – it's been a couple of minutes since I last looked at the window, but I can hear the wind whistling. Even through these thick walls, it's loud enough to make me nervous.

Nora is in the kitchen, cutting up onions while her eyes water. She sniffs, sees me, then turns her back to me and hunches over the chopping board. It takes a few seconds to realise, and my heart sinks as soon as it registers.

She's cutting carrots, not onions.

And those tears are her own.

'Nora?' I say, moving to her side and letting her know I can see what's happening.

'What are you doing here?' she asks. 'You're supposed to be upstairs, teaching.'

Although she says it moodily, I'm not buying it. This woman has never been anything but nice to me, and it will take more than one badly acted, miserable question to hide whatever it is she's feeling. I stand my ground on this, getting closer so she knows I won't back down.

'What happened?' I ask.

'It's nothing.'

'If it was nothing, then you wouldn't be cry—'

My words stumble to a stop when I spot it. Her sweatshirt is yellow with swirls of bright red, so it's hard to see at first. But when I lean in close and study, it's easy to discern the difference between the red pattern... and the splash of blood on her shoulder.

'Nora, did he hurt you?'

'Just leave it alone.' She continues to chop carrots, the tears still coming.

'That's easier said than done.' I sigh and look out the nearest window. The snow is picking up, coming down in flurries and starting to settle. How long will it be before I'm snowed in up here? How much time do I have to make my escape?

Moving slowly so as not to startle her, I take the knife from her hand and set it to one side. She cries harder then, using her knuckles to dry her eyes. I hush her like a mother would an injured child. 'Show me,' I say, helping her unzip the sweatshirt.

She nervously shrugs it off and pulls aside the strap of the top underneath. There's a strip of gauze taped to her shoulder, but the scarlet seeping through proves it's done a lousy job.

'Shit,' I mutter, now facing a dilemma.

I hope it's not selfish that I want to go home. I *really* do. But how can any rational woman leave Nora up here alone while she's getting cut up like the carrots she was just going to town on? It's not a dilemma – not even close – because the humane side of me won't stand to see another woman treated this way.

'Did Richard do this to you?' I ask, already knowing the answer.

'It's my fault,' she says. 'I answered him back.'

'That doesn't give him the right. What happened?'

Nora shakes her head and wipes her eyes again while I pull the first aid box off the wall and start patching her up properly. I start by peeling the old gauze away from the skin. The cut isn't too deep, but Nora still hisses while I do it.

'Richard is in a bad mood, as usual,' she says, trying to look away while I clean up the bloody mess. 'Apparently, he has some online client meetings all afternoon and asked if he could have dinner a little sooner. I told him there were still some chores to do before I could even think about cooking, and he didn't like the answer.'

'Then what?'

'He told me to make a miracle happen.'

'What did you say to that?'

'It's not important.'

'What did you say to that?' I ask again, wondering what could possibly have upset him enough that he started cutting her. I'm unsure if I want to shout at her for letting him do it or hug her because he did. Nobody deserves to be treated like this.

'I told him he could cook his own damn dinner.'

I stop, looking up at her with a roll of medical tape in my hand. 'That's it?'

'Yes. That's when he grabbed the letter opener and swiped at me.'

'He cut you just because he couldn't eat soon enough?'

Nora nods, glances at her wound as best she can, then looks away with a grimace.

There's nothing else to say, but my heart is racing with rage. If anything should make me tell her to pack up and come down the hill, this is it. Believe me, I have every mind to march upstairs and yell him into a corner, but I'm smart enough to know better. Men like Richard are dangerous – they don't have morals or self-control. They act on their emotions, and nothing could ensure a quicker death than shouting at him that he's done something wrong.

Then I wonder... is this exactly what happened to Katie?

'You have to do something about this,' I tell Nora matter-of-factly.

'That's a bad idea. It will only make him angrier.'

'But this is bodily harm.' I point at the wound I just finished dressing.

Nora pulls her sweatshirt back on and backs away. 'It doesn't matter. He doesn't care.'

'Well, he *should* bloody care.'

'Leave it alone. Please.'

'Absolutely not. This needs to be reported.'

'What does?' comes a deep, dominant voice from beside us.

Nora and I both spin around to see Richard standing there, filling up the doorway with his huge body. It perfectly illustrates his size, which makes confronting him even harder. Words fail me. Nora hurries back to her chopping board, like an ostrich burying her head in the sand. I, however, am stuck there, frozen to the spot with the dilemma of whether or not to address it.

'Well?' he says, demanding a response.

I envision a fork in the road: do I make up an answer to keep him at bay or stand up for what's right and risk all hell breaking loose? It feels like either answer is wrong, but the words are out of my mouth before I can even process them.

'The weather,' I say, instantly feeling my body flush with regret and weakness. 'The snow is coming down pretty heavy. Couriers and taxis are going to have a hard time on the roads, so I think they should be reporting it on the radio.'

Richard eyes me in the awkward silence. He looks to Nora, who is now scraping sliced carrot into a mixing bowl with leafy greens. His gaze lingers on her for a few seconds while I try talking myself into confronting him for what he just did. The problem is, I can see him unleashing his fury, attacking me, Nora, or perhaps even his own son. Is that the real reason I don't say anything, or am I just a coward hiding behind a flimsy excuse?

'You're right,' he says, then moves between us on his way to the window. I pivot to face him, refusing to have my back to him at any time. He stands there, watching the snow come down like white, frothy rain. Just like I did just a few minutes ago. Although even from here, I can see it's getting heavier. 'I have some bad news for you, Emma.'

My heart sinks into my stomach. 'What's that?'

'You're not going anywhere.'

Suddenly, I look at Nora. She pauses in the middle of her cooking duties but doesn't say anything. I swing back around to see Richard, who's now looking right at me with a massive grin on his face. It should be lifting my spirits, but he just looks menacing.

'See how thick it is?' he says, pointing at the window. 'There's not a hope in hell of you getting back down this hill with all that going on outside. The good news is that we have plenty of space in the house for you to stay here until it thaws.'

'Oh. No, I couldn't,' I say, panicking.

'You don't have a choice.'

'I don't mind risking it.'

Richard sighs audibly, stepping aside. 'See for yourself.'

Hesitantly, I stroll across the kitchen towards him, then peer through the glass. The snow is carpeting the ground, reaching the bottom post of the fences outside. Snow that thick will reach my shins, maybe even higher than that, and it's only getting thicker by the second. I think back to my previous trips up and down the hill – it was a struggle even then. But now?

I hate to say it, but he's right.

'It's not the end of the world,' he tries assuring me, as if he hasn't been beating and cutting his own wife. 'You can have your own room. Nora can cook for you, and I'm sure she won't mind sharing some of her spare clothes. Would you, Nora?'

Nora shakes her head but doesn't turn around.

I'm in a bad place now. Worse than before. Not

only has Richard's hold on Nora got fiercer, but now I'm stuck in the middle of it all. Even if I wanted to break my promise to Nora and report all this to the police, there's no way I could. This house has no Wi-Fi, I have no phone, and we're stuck on a hill outside of town.

In layman's terms, I'm screwed.

Richard's smile is a half sneer. 'Welcome to the family,' he says.

Chapter Nine

It's been two days since I last saw Richard, and the snow isn't getting any lighter. Each time I look out the window, it seems to have built up by yet another inch. At this rate, it shouldn't be long before the whole town is swamped in it. In fact, if I look from my upstairs bedroom – far superior to my room at the bed and breakfast, by the way, even if it is significantly less safe – I can see kids throwing snowballs and sledging down small mounds. It makes me wish I was with them, playing down there rather than being stuck up here.

At least tutoring is going well. Richard and Nora decided together that Jacob isn't to waste his days playing out in the snow and that they should all make use of me being here. I saw the pain in his eyes when his mother told him that, and I felt really sorry for him. Even in the north of England, it doesn't snow that often. How many more times is he really going to get this chance? Even if he does, I doubt it will be this thick again.

To his credit, Jacob didn't whine. He simply accepted his dissatisfaction and made his way back to the kitchen, where he sat at the island to eat his tuna and cucumber sandwich in silence. I'm actually a little jealous, as my appetite has left a lot to be desired since I got locked in here. Nevertheless, I've been helping Nora cook and take care of a couple of chores here and there. I just hope Richard has no complaints about that.

As Jacob is all tied up and I don't feel like eating, I throw on my coat and boots before stepping outside to find Nora on the back patio. She has another cigarette pinched between her frost-pinked fingers, and she's staring out into space again. I approach slowly and carefully, hoping not to startle (and possibly even traumatise) the poor woman – it's convenient that her husband is a doctor, but it seems she'd rather die than have him take care of her.

'Nora?' I say in a low breath. 'Can we talk?'

Nora pivots around and offers a thin smile. 'Right now?'

'It's nothing to worry about. I was just wondering how your wound is doing.'

'Oh, it causes a little sting from time to time, but it's all right.'

My head bobs slowly up and down as I approach her solemnly. Nora's hand reaches out, a pack of cigarettes clutched in them. I haven't smoked since I was eighteen years old, and I'm not about to start again. I shake my head, and Nora puts the pack away.

'You know, I've lived here for years and never once set foot in those woods.' Nora nods towards the expansive range of trees that sits at the back of her snow-blanketed garden. It's still coming down heavily, the sunlight bouncing off the bare, white branches to make it look like some kind of enchanted forest. 'I should learn to appreciate the little things.'

I shrug. 'There's something to be said for staying in your comfort zone.'

'Is that what you think it is? My comfort zone?'

'Not to be too judgemental, but it seems like you don't enjoy rocking the boat.'

'That's a fair assessment.'

Nora takes a long drag of her cancer stick and blows it out. A grey cloud expels into the air like smog from a ship's funnel. It dissipates within seconds, but I can still smell it.

'Do you think you'll ever leave this place?' I ask.

'Do you mean with or without Richard?'

'Either.'

'I honestly don't think he'll let me.'

'This isn't my business, but... isn't that more of a reason to go?'

Nora treads past me, her footfalls crunching in the snow like she's stamping on glass. She pulls out the secret coffee jar and dumps her disused cigarette into it. 'You're right, it's not your business. I sincerely thank you for helping me, but I don't want to anger my husband.'

'Yeah, I'm sorry.' I take a deep breath and blow out a cloud of my own. 'It's ultimately your decision, but I want you to know that you're not alone in this. He hurts you, Nora, and you deserve better. So if you ever want help getting away, I'm right here.'

Nora smiles, and I have no idea how genuine it is. I know I'm crossing boundaries, but there's a very humane part of me that can't resist trying to save someone who clearly needs to be saved. Not that she can see it for herself — she's already heading back inside without another word. It makes me wonder if she'll ever put her foot down on this.

But I suppose we had it right before. It's not my business — as long as I'm safe and Jacob isn't getting caught up in all this, there's nothing I can do but sit back and wait until things get too out of hand. And given how things ended up with Katie, who knows what will happen then?

All I know is that the air has suddenly got even colder.

IF I'M BEING COMPLETELY honest, I don't feel like going back inside yet. I've felt so isolated recently that even the freezing air feels nice and fresh. I take a few moments to soak it in, closing my eyes against the sunlight and inhaling deeply.

This is the calmest I've felt in over a week.

I'm technically on my lunch break, and I've been told more than once that I'm free to explore the house and grounds as much as I see fit.

Although this tells me there's nothing to hide, it still has my curiosity. I mean, as it stands, this is my temporary home.

I begin by walking the perimeter of the house, sticking close to the wall until I've done an entire lap. Even this takes five to ten minutes, and I was distracted the whole time by the woods, an old well, and a large structure that looks like an oddly shaped barn. After my first lap, I head for that barn for a closer look, stomping through the snow and losing the bottom half of my legs with each step. My toes are numb, and it's like they're not even there any more, but that's okay – I'll warm them up when I get back inside.

The barn is large and unused, with holes in the unpainted wood and a door that's creaking slightly open and shut in the wind. I look back at the house, wondering if I'm being watched from one of the many windows. What will I find in here, I ask myself? Hay? Carpentry tools and storage boxes that have been banned from the house?

Katie?

I take a deep, steadying breath and reach for the door. It opens easily into the dark interior, and I step inside. My nerves are getting the better of me, but I fight through and walk further in, instantly assaulted by a grassy smell I can only assume is straw. The open door casts enough light to see right to the back, and although there are little bays on either side where I presume animals once lived, they're now completely empty.

There's nothing here.

Is it weird that I feel disappointed? I was kind of hoping to find some answers – to stumble upon my predecessor either living or dead. That's the part of me that loves stories, I suppose. I want a good reason to risk walking down the hill. That's how desperate I'm starting to feel, but although it's dangerous, I have to wonder...

Is it any safer to stay up here?

When I make it back to the house, all the attention is on me.

Richard is standing by the back door, blocking my entry. His eyes are piercing right through me, my legs turning to jelly. He watches me come in, and Nora is at his side. She's looking at me with the expression of a woman who needs something – her wide eyes pleading me for help without a single word leaving her lips.

'Do you have something to tell me?' he says.

All of a sudden, I feel like a young pupil. Richard is like the scary teacher who has me backed into a corner, mere seconds away from scolding me for whatever it is I'm supposed to have done. And just like the technique I've used myself in the past, he's giving me a chance to confess my sins, thus reducing my punishment.

'I don't know,' I tell him honestly. 'Have I done something wrong?'

My mind is racing, scanning through the events of the morning as if it's a greatest hits collection. Did I use the wrong words around Jacob? Have I taught him things that are forbidden in this house, unbeknownst to me?

'Last chance to admit it,' he says.

I swallow a dry lump and consider the consequences. There's no way out of this. I'm about to be punished, and I don't even know what for. I look at Nora, her expression unchanged. My gaze falls to a small item in Richard's hand. I can only see a small blue piece of card with a subtle touch of foil. I think I recognise it and rack my brain to figure out why.

Then, it all falls into place.

'I was smoking,' I say, taking the fall for Nora. 'Is that not allowed here?'

Nora's body sags with relief.

Richard, on the other hand, puffs his chest out, anger taking over his posture as he seems to grow a couple of inches. If I thought he was intimidating before, now he's somehow managed to get worse. The man before me knows he has authority, and he's not afraid to assert it. Even if it is with a woman he barely knows.

'It absolutely is *not* okay,' he says. 'Not only do we have a young child in this house, but I have a wife. Do you think I want her to walk around the house with your dirty cigarette smoke sunk into the fabric of her clothes? It stinks, Emma, and I don't like it.'

I don't like being berated, especially for something I didn't do, but from what I've seen, it's got to be better than what he'd do to Nora if he knew the truth. Is he really so controlling that he won't even let his own wife smoke? Judging from the fear and panic in her eyes, I'd imagine they've had this conversation more than once.

Who can blame her for not wanting to get cut again?

'I'm sorry,' is all I can think to say, lowering my head like a sulking child.

'"Sorry" isn't good enough, I'm afraid. You'll need to promise me you won't smoke on this property ever again, starting from today. Promise me, Emma, and whatever you do, don't you dare break that promise.'

'I won't smoke again,' I tell him loud and clear. 'I promise.'

Nora starts biting her nails, looking up at her husband from his side. I stand there in the silence, my feet still burning with cold from the deep snow. I play with the idea of telling him about the coffee jar full of cigarette butts, just in case he finds it and hits the roof.

But honestly, I'm too scared.

'Good,' he says after an agonising wait. 'Don't let me catch you doing that again.'

On his way out of the room, he scrunches the cigarette pack in his massive hand and hurls it into the bin. It's no surprise he hates smokers so much – he's a doctor, after all – but for him to act so aggressively towards me for something I didn't even know was wrong...

'Sorry,' I say one more time, but Richard doesn't look at me before leaving the room.

Nora rushes towards me, slinging her arms over my shoulders. She holds on tight, clutching the back of my coat and thanking me with her weak, scattered breath. Anyone would think I've just saved her life by taking the blame for her smoking.

Who knows – maybe I have.

Chapter Ten

First thing the next morning, Jacob is on a high.

Not only has he managed to pass his latest test with flying colours, but he's also been spending his evenings reading aloud in his room. I questioned this, of course, asking what his mother and father do during this time, to which he responds that they pretty much do their own thing in one of the living rooms. I can't help but scoff jealously.

"One of."

At least he's being taken care of with the basics. Dinner time is at six o'clock, bath time is at seven, and the reading is done in broken portions between and after those things. I'm actually incredibly proud to see he's spending his spare time educating himself. It's all fiction, but reading is reading, and that's never a bad thing.

'I want to show off to Mummy and Daddy,' he suddenly looks up to confess in the middle of a lesson. He's looking up at me with such excitement, a smile bursting onto his face as if he's finally going to get the approval he deserves. Something tells me he won't.

At least not from his father.

'Do you think it's good enough for that?' he prompts through my silence.

'Oh. Yes, sweetie, I think you're doing brilliantly.'

'So can I show them?'

It's not that I think he isn't a strong reader – he really is, especially for his age – but I don't want him getting hurt. Nora is a good mother, but I rarely see her interact with her own son. And with the way Richard's been acting, I'd be shocked for him to suddenly take an interest. After all, has he ever been anything other than stern?

'Now might not be a good time,' I say, letting Jacob down lightly. 'You're *really* good at reading, and at listening, and your memory is excellent. But your mum and dad are very busy people, and they might not have time to sit through a reading.'

Jacob shrinks with disappointment, and the guilt tears me apart.

Then I get another idea. It's not much, but it's something.

'How about this,' I say in my most soothing tone. 'We can take the week to prepare something special for them. Give them time to work it into their schedules. Then we can sit down in front of your parents and read a whole chapter to them. Maybe even more.'

'But I want to do it now.'

'It's just not a good time.'

Jacob crosses his arms. 'Why not?'

'Because...' I don't have a good reason. At least not without telling him the truth about his parents: Nora is constantly busy with housework, and Richard doesn't seem to give a damn about anything except working in the confines of his office and occasionally stepping out to give his own wife some disciplinary action.

'Because what?' Jacob urges.

I give in with a breezing sigh. 'Okay, let's do it.'

My star (and only) pupil leaps out of his seat and runs to his bookshelf. Ignoring the book he's currently in the middle of reading, he pulls a fresh one off the shelf, examines it quickly, then hurries back to me with all the giddiness in the world.

'Ready to go?' I ask.

'Yep!'

He reaches for my hand, and I'm nervous about how this will go down. Maybe it could be a surprise, and his parents will be delighted to learn their son wants to show off his latest developments. I walk him through the long, winding hallways of the house, looking for his mother, and we're lucky enough to find two for the price of one in the upstairs study.

'Mum! Dad!' he yells, running in.

Nora and Richard are standing together by a large oak desk. Nora has her arms folded and her head hung low – a sight I'm becoming all too familiar with. Richard, strong and imposing as ever, is staring at us with eyes like little hot coals. One thing is immediately clear.

He doesn't appreciate the interruption.

'This had better be important,' Richard says.

'It is.' Jacob runs over to them, book in hand. 'Look, I'm getting really good at reading!'

'That's really good, son, but now's not a good time.'

My heart collapses on itself as I feel Jacob's

young soul breaking. The room goes dead silent, awkwardness filling it like a flood. Richard towers over his only child, who stares down at his book. Nora doesn't move – as usual, she's like a deer in headlights. I can only imagine she *wants* to hear her son read, but honestly?

It doesn't seem like she's allowed to.

'Okay,' Jacob says flatly, leaving the room without me.

I'm left alone with the boy's parents, but not a single word is said between us. It doesn't need to be, as all three of us are communicating with our eyes. It's easy enough to read what we're all thinking: Nora is upset, Richard is angry for the interruption, and if my face displays my true feelings, it's casting shame and disappointment.

A second later, I leave the room.

It's been a rough day, and I feel it in my dry eyes.

Nora took care of me for dinner, but I was told to eat it in the kitchen alone once again. I assume this is her way of keeping business and her family life entirely separate, but I know she's a warm, giving person, and I don't doubt for a second that it was Richard's idea to keep this arrangement. I don't mind that much; I'm too tired to perform as a good or interesting dinner guest. So I ate, helped clear up the mess in the kitchen, then retired to my room.

I don't like it in here. It's a beautiful room with a white marble fireplace that may or may not be for aesthetics only. The king-size bed is so soft I could probably get lost in the folds of mattress when my body sinks into it. There's an amazing view of Wedchester from the window, with the deep snow so white it no longer looks like night. The whole world seems bright down in that cosy little town, but up here?

Everything seems dark.

I'm trying not to think about the situation with this family, diving into my workbooks and trying to get ahead of myself as much as possible. Jacob's schedule has now been prepared for an entire week, which makes me question if I'll still be here by then. Teaching, most probably, but if there truly is a God, he'll at least melt the snow and let me leave. I feel a little like Rapunzel, locked away from the outside world.

I can't remember, does she have a happy ending?

There's no noise up here either. No sounds reach us from the town, and I can't even hear the family moving around. The house is too big, the hallways too long for the sound to travel. I should be hearing Jacob running around after his bath. There should be the patter of footsteps up and down the corridor as Nora and Richard find their way to bed.

Do they even sleep together, I wonder?

It doesn't matter. It's not my business. All I have to worry about is getting myself to sleep in this unfamiliar territory. With a bed this comfortable in a room this warm, it shouldn't be a problem at all. Yet, as I lie here in the dark silence with my mind racing, all I keep thinking is that I'm currently at my most vulnerable – in here, Richard could easily hurt me.

And nobody would ever know.

When I do finally get to sleep, I'm dreaming about doors.

It's not the most normal thing to dream about, I admit, but the brain wants what it wants. I've done a lot of reading on dreams over the years – my mother was obsessed with oneirology and baited me into it – so I know exactly what this dream means.

I'm staring at an enormous red door. There are bars on the windows, and I can't get in. If my memory serves, doors represent arising opportunities and challenges. It's easy to put together that my brain is making a big deal of the job I recently stumbled upon. But the red?

The red suggests danger.

Even in the dream world, I can put two and two together. Although the door looks like an average, everyday door, it's more like the entrance to a jail cell. Perhaps even the *exit*, depending on your perspective. I'm trying to push against it, to open it and get through, but it won't budge. I'm weightless. Helpless.

Stuck.

When I look down, I see a letter box I didn't notice before. It's gleaming white, almost luminescent, as if God himself has granted it some kind of holy power. I stop pushing against the door and get to my knees. It won't let me touch it. It's as if two magnets are getting pushed together, my hand swaying to one side each time I try. What does this mean, and why can't I get to it? Even when I lie on my side and dig my shoulder into the ground for leverage, the letter box refuses to let me near as it flickers from light to dark, light to dark.

It's only a matter of time before I realise.

The letter box is my window to the real world.

My eyes slowly flicker open, melding the shapes in my dream with the light under the real-life bedroom door. I'm so exhausted that I can't quite figure out if my imagination is still making stuff up, so I sit up and squint into the darkness while my brain adjusts to the late hour.

It's not a letter box. I can see that now. A light is on in the hallway, a small beam of yellow spreading across the bottom of the door. But it's not the light that woke me – that's a steady state, only fluctuating when the source is interrupted. It's the blinking that's making my heart beat so rapidly, my groggy mind finally understanding what's going on.

Someone is outside my door.

'Hello?' I say, daring my midnight visitor to reveal themselves.

Reveal *him*self.

I know it's not Nora. If she wanted something from me, I truly believe she would simply enter and ask for what she needs. I'm convinced it's Richard out in the hall, unless I've well and truly lost it and can make myself believe Katie is alive –

that she's escaped from whatever hell she's been lost in and has come by my room to warn me. Maybe even rescue me.

'Is someone there?' I try, losing my nerve as the feet shuffle merely metres away.

There's no response. Not a peep. But the figure does shift at the sound of my voice, eventually clearing out of the way and allowing the beam of light to fully restore itself. I'm too scared to move, fear seizing me on the spot. But if I'm ever going to unravel this mystery, I have to cross the room and open the door without further delay.

I don't think about it. I throw the duvet across the bed and shoot to my feet, rushing for the door. The handle whines as I tear the door open, half expecting to come face to face with Richard as he punishes me for smoking on his property or for helping his wife.

But nobody is there.

Am I going mad, or did my visitor simply flee the scene before I could catch him? There's no way to know for sure as the hallway is completely vacant, the two light bulbs shining down on the hardwood floors as if to emphasise its own emptiness.

Whoever I saw – or *thought* I saw – is gone.

What I'm left with is a profound sense of invasion, my only private space in the entire world breached at the least convenient hour. What would have happened if I didn't wake up? Would he have come in if I didn't call out to him?

Maybe I'll never know.

Maybe I'll find out the hard way.

Chapter Eleven

NEEDLESS TO SAY, the rest of the night is sleepless. I can't help watching the door, thinking someone is about to come in and continue with whatever it was they were thinking of doing. Some might call this paranoia – some irrational behaviour – but I just think it's good sense.

As soon as the sun rises, I throw on yesterday's clothes with only a change of underwear, saving Nora the pain of doing my laundry. I spray a bit of deodorant, then head downstairs to the kitchen, where the enticing aroma of cooking meat fills the air.

Nora is in here, working the frying pan with black bags under her eyes as bacon sizzles in front of her. Jacob is sitting on the too-tall stool by the island, lazily scooping scrambled eggs onto his fork before shakily transferring them into his mouth. Even with a full mouth, he tries to smile at me as I come in and sit beside him, holding back a yawn.

'Morning, all,' I say.

Nora looks over her shoulder. 'Good morning, Emma. How did you sleep?'

'Not well, actually. I was up all night.'

'You and me both. Must be something in the air.'

Jacob drops the fork onto his plate and carries it over to the dishwasher, putting away his own things before returning to tug on my sleeve. 'What subjects are we doing today?'

'A bit of history. The Tudors – fun stuff.'

'What's a Tudor?'

'You'll soon find out.'

Jacob grins a cheeky, gap-toothed smile. 'Mum, can I read in my room while I wait?'

'Did you finish your breakfast?' Nora asks.

'Uh-huh.'

'Then I don't see why not.'

After shooting me a goofy little grin – which I happily return – Jacob runs out of the room as if he's been challenged to a race. His footsteps patter up the hall before fading into nothingness, leaving

Nora and me completely alone. She doesn't say anything to me, even as she serves up some bacon and sausages with a slice of toast. I thank her for putting in the effort, then watch as she goes back to whizz around the kitchen like a professional chef.

I'm watching her, of course. Her body language. The way she looks at me occasionally. The way she doesn't. I'm trying to figure out if she looks guilty of something – like coming to visit my room in the middle of the night – or if I'm looking way too far into this.

There's only one way to find out.

'What time did you go to bed?' I say, not so much as looking at my breakfast.

'Hmm. Probably not until around ten. Why do you ask?'

'Well, somebody was standing outside my door.'

'Are you sure?'

'Certain.'

'What time?'

'A little after two in the morning.'

Nora drops a pan into the sink. It hisses as steam waves towards the ceiling. She turns and leans against the counter. 'No, that wasn't me. I doubt it was Richard either. I'm a very light sleeper and would have noticed him getting out of bed.'

That only leaves Jacob, I think. *But why would he come to see me?*

Before I can say any more, Richard makes an appearance in the kitchen. He's wearing an expensive-looking white shirt that's tucked in as if he's actually leaving the house for once. But as he comes around the island, I see he's wearing his slippers. He isn't going anywhere.

No surprise.

'What are you ladies gossiping about?' he asks, sparing us a simple hello.

I get a brief glance across the kitchen from Nora before she turns and wipes the pan in the sink, then moves to the dishwasher to slide it in. 'Emma was just telling me about the week she has planned. It seems our son is getting a decent education from her.'

Richard glares at me briefly, filling his mug from the coffee machine. He grunts like some kind of brute who's barely satisfied with the answer he was given, takes a small sip of coffee, then heads for the door without another word. I wait a minute to make sure the coast is clear, then look at Nora. She doesn't remark on the abruptness of his visit, but then again, she's had many more years to adapt to his behaviour.

For me, this is brand new. Richard hasn't said more to me than he has to, which is a dead giveaway that he's a cold, rude human being with very little appreciation for the woman schooling his kid. I did think about asking if it was him who came to my room, but there's a reason I didn't. Even though it's hard to admit to myself, it can't be denied.

The truth is, I'm scared of him.

AFTER BREAKFAST, I find Jacob lying at the top of the stairs. He's on his back, one leg kicked over the other and swinging as he holds a book above his head. I stop to watch him, proud to have instilled a little happiness in an otherwise moody young boy. Not that I'm going to kid myself – it's literature that made him this happy.

It does that to most of us.

He's so engaged in his story that he hasn't even realised I'm here. I enjoy the sight for a few more seconds, the grandfather clock echoing dully through the hall, then clear my throat. Jacob rotates his head and spots me, gets up lazily as if his body has no bones, then stands aside as I rise up the stairs to meet him.

'You ready to get started?' I ask.

'Yep!'

Without warning, he bounds down the hallway towards his bedroom. I follow after him, stop by my room just briefly to grab my things, then meet him at the table where we usually study. I wish my previous students were this eager.

Most of the morning goes by quickly, but I'm a little distracted by the view from his window. The snow is still falling, which has to be some kind of record. I'm starting to think I'll never get out of here – that the snow will outlast even me, if Katie's disappearance is anything to go by. It's that line of thought that leads me back around to last night's events. The vulnerability returns to me like a boomerang.

'Jacob,' I say, turning to distract him from his work.

'What?'

'I don't suppose you came by my room last night?'

'Yeah. I didn't knock though.'

I shake my head and smile, assuring him he's in no trouble for it. If anything, I'm just relieved it wasn't Richard. My skin has been in goosebumps ever since it happened. Just the thought of that overbearing man coming to see me in the dead of night burdens me with fear so deep I haven't been able to shake it off.

Until now.

'Whatever possessed you to sneak around the house at night?' I ask, coming to join him at the table. I pull aside one of the small chairs meant for children, drag out a beanbag, then plonk down into it. 'You could have stumbled in the dark and hurt yourself.'

'Not really. I do it all the time.'

'You do?'

Jacob bobs his head in a half nod, his eyes not leaving the book he's keeping a finger pointed at just so he doesn't lose his place. For half a second, he looks like an adult. 'Katie used to let me stay with her all the time. I have trouble sleeping, so she would keep me safe.'

'Safe from what?'

'I don't know. Monsters?'

'There's no such thing as monsters.' I laugh with him, not at him. 'But if you ever get scared in the night again, you just come and knock on my door, okay?'

Jacob looks up at me, smiles, then returns to the book. I watch him for a minute, wondering if I can push this further than I should. The more I hear about Katie, the more I want to learn about her disappearance. Selfishly, that could just be because I want to know what kind of situation I'm in. If Richard really did do something to her, I'd like to find out about it.

Sooner rather than later.

'Do you miss her?' I ask.

'Katie?'

'Yes.'

'Sometimes. She was good at teaching me stuff. Not as good as you, but she was really nice. It would be really amazing if I can have you both as teachers. Not just as teachers though, but friends as well. You're both really nice.'

I beam at him but stay focused. 'What do you think happened to her?'

'I don't know. Mummy says she's not coming back.'

'Is that why you drew her grave?'

Jacob raises his shoulders, half shrugging. 'It just felt right.'

If a comment like that doesn't unnerve me, I would officially have balls of steel. Kids say the creepiest things, and I'm too nervous to get any more out of him. Perhaps Jacob is smarter than he thinks – he might have subconsciously picked up on some unclean air between Katie and Richard, which only came out when he sat down to create that drawing. It would explain why he doesn't seem to know much more.

Doesn't know... or isn't allowed to say.

AFTER THE DAY'S SESSION, I stretch my legs by wandering the halls of the house. When it starts to feel a little restrictive, I put on my coat and step out into the bitter air, taking a stroll around the outside once more. The grounds are massive – way too big for a family of three – but it looks beautiful in the January sunset. A sheet of orange is cast across the sky, lighting up the snow like a bed of crystals. Most people I know would be rushing to take a photo.

I just want to admire it.

Standing in one spot to gaze out at the view of the town, I wonder just how hard it would be to make the trip. An absolute nightmare, I'm willing to bet, but I'd give anything to sit in the local pub with a glass of wine and start telling people the things I've seen. I wouldn't, of course, even if I could. Things like that tend to backfire, as it likely did with Katie.

She's all I can think about. No matter how hard I try, my head is swimming with theories about her disappearance. The police may not have found anything, but I've seen enough of Richard to know he has a temper. I've seen enough of *Nora* to be certain of his violent streak. You might think it's none of my business what happened to the other tutor, but if my safety is at risk, then I don't just want to know.

I *need* to know.

But asking about it is sure to piss some people off. Jacob has told me everything there is to say on the matter, and there's not a chance in hell of asking Richard. That's a sure-fire way to terminate my employment – and possibly my life – almost instantly.

Nora, on the other hand...

She's a vulnerable woman. The idea of escaping this marriage must be appealing to her, but she's so damn scared of her husband that she won't give up even the slightest details about Richard, much less Katie.

Well, that ends tomorrow.

As soon as I can catch her alone, I'm going to put her on the spot and ask for the truth. After everything that's happened between her and Richard – between *me* and Richard – the least I deserve is a fragment of truth about the mystery.

She must know the whole town is talking about it.

It's decided. No matter how scary it might be to approach the subject, it's scarier to not know. As I make my way back towards the door for another night in what – for all I know – could be some kind of murder house, I make myself the promise that tomorrow will reveal all.

I *will* get answers.

Chapter Twelve

Jacob has yet another test today. Nothing official, but enough to give me some time alone with Nora. The problem is, I haven't seen her all day. I've only seen Richard, who gave nothing but an unhappy grunt as we crossed paths in the kitchen. Despite trying to be friendly with him, he didn't give me so much as a single word before walking off into the corridor, crunching on an apple while he disappeared.

'I'll be right back,' I tell Jacob, looking at my watch. 'You have thirty minutes.'

'Can I read some of my book?'

'Only when you finish the test. Every single question, okay?'

Jacob flips over the page and grabs a pencil,

getting to work while his tongue hangs out of his mouth. I guess his time begins now, so I check my watch again and note the time, then head out of the door and close it behind me.

So begins my search for Nora.

I start on the upper floor, knocking on the doors of every room I'm allowed in and then allowing myself entry – just enough to poke my head in the door and take a quick scan around. She's not in any of those, which is starting to have me a little worried. There are plenty more rooms that I'm *not* allowed in, but I know better than to check those.

After that, I make my way downstairs and try again, checking in the kitchen first (that's where I usually find Nora) and then the back patio. There's no sign of her whatsoever – it's almost as if she never lived here in the first place. When I've checked all of the downstairs rooms and even taken a quick look out in the snow, there's only one thing I can do.

I have to ask Richard.

It's not my brightest idea, but my breath is becoming shallower at the thought of something happening to Nora. What if something happened to her overnight? What if she's suffered the same fate as Katie, whatever that is? Fear overwhelms me as I realise Jacob could be drawing a picture of *her* grave soon. Then what?

Would I be next?

By the time I gather the courage to knock on Richard's office door, fifteen minutes have passed. Jacob must be over halfway through his test by now, hopefully working his way towards being able to read a book. It relieves some of the guilt I feel for leaving him.

I only knock twice, feeling awful for disturbing Richard. After a short wait, he rips open the door and stares down at me like I've just crashed his wedding. His eyes are bloodshot with the toll of fatigue, and I can't remember if they were like that earlier.

'There's a do-not-disturb rule on this room,' he says. 'Should I buy a sign?'

'Sorry,' I tell him, 'but I need to speak with Nora and can't find her anywhere.'

'Have you tried the kitchen?'

'Yes, she's not there.'

'Any of the other rooms?'

'I've tried all the ones I'm allowed near.'

Richard rubs his temples like he's in physical pain, his eyes closing as he thinks about where his wife might have gone. 'Last time I saw her was a couple of hours ago, when she was in bed. Try the master bedroom. Upstairs, third door on the left.'

The door slams in my face, making me leap back as my heart skips a beat. Now that I have his advice and permission to enter their bedroom, it's more or less confirmed that I'm not doing anything wrong. I head up there as quickly as possible, rap on the door, then begin to worry when it opens under the force of my knock.

'Nora?' I say, easing it open. 'Are you in here?'

She doesn't reply, but I hear a whimper from the en suite. I don't care if this is forbidden – I step inside and cross the room to the inner door. Peering inside, I gasp as I find Nora in the worst state imaginable; she's leaning over the sink, her dark eyes a marriage of black and blue, blood covering her nose and smeared down her chin as she tries to wipe it away with a trembling hand. Her eyes dart to me as I come in, and then – as if she's been holding it in all morning – she drops the cotton ball into the sink.

And bursts into tears.

'Oh, my God,' I say in a weak breath.

Nora weeps as I run forward, throwing my arms around her and letting her cry. I don't care that she's getting blood all over my blouse – I hold her close and let her know she's not alone in this. There is never an excuse for domestic abuse, verbally or – in this case – physically. Trust me, I've been there. It can feel so isolating and painful. Not just the damage they cause instantly but with the lies and deceit that follow.

She's not going to go through this alone.

Not if I can help it.

I stroke her hair and peel away from her, asking her to tilt back her head so I can get a good look. There's some serious damage to her face. It doesn't look like enough to take her to the hospital (wherever the nearest one is), but this is going to sting for more than just a couple of days. Taking into account Richard's size, it seems as though he only hit her once.

It's hard to tell if that's something to be grateful for.

I get to work on cleaning her up, using wipes and cotton balls soaked in alcohol. Nora sits on the lid of the toilet seat, her bottom lip still quivering so fast it looks like it's vibrating. She winces when I apply the alcohol, but it's a necessary evil.

'What happened?' I ask.

'I fell.'

'The truth, please. I wasn't born yesterday.'

Nora pauses while I focus on cleaning her wound, then gives in. 'Richard said he was sick of the sight of me. That all he does is work, and all I do is potter around the house like some depressed widow.'

My head shakes with disgust before I can stop it, but I don't interrupt.

'Then he told me to stay in the room until he says otherwise. I tried telling him, Emma.' Nora grabs my arms as she begins to cry all over again. 'I tried telling him the house doesn't take care of itself. Jacob needs lunch. *Richard* needs lunch, and he'd probably hit me again if I didn't sort that out for him on time. But he said he didn't care and that I had to stay.'

'I wondered where you were this morning.'

'Sorry I wasn't there to make you breakfast.'

'Don't be silly.'

There are a few moments of silence while I wipe away a smear of blood. I take a glance at my watch and realise Jacob has been alone for over thirty minutes. Guilt tugs at my heartstrings, but I hope he's content with his book. As excuses go for me not being there…

'I left the room anyway,' Nora goes on. 'Mostly just to get some chores done. But then he caught me, dragged me back to this room, and told me I'd get what I deserve. That's when he pinned me against the wall and…'

The wound is clean now, her nose wiped dry of blood, so I hold her close again. I don't want to tell her that her usually pleasant face is now an explosion of colour. Not the good kind either. As I hug her tight, feeling her hands grasp the back of my blouse, I decide to take the responsibility of saying more than what is considered acceptable.

'You need to report this,' I say with as little emotion as possible. 'This isn't right.'

'But he'll hurt me. You know that.'

'With all due respect, what do you think he's already doing?'

Nora doesn't answer, and once again, I find myself thinking about Katie. There has never been a less appropriate time to start pressing for answers, but Richard's violent side is nothing if not obvious, so the mystery sort of resolves itself in my mind.

Katie is gone, and Richard is the one who *made* her gone.

'You need help,' I whisper in Nora's ear. 'I'm going to get you help.'

'Please don't. I'm scared, Emma.'

'I know, but you won't have to be scared for much longer.'

'No, you don't understand how dangerous he is. He—'

Nora's words are cut off by an explosion of sound. The door smashes open and strikes the wall. A shadow stretches across the bathroom, a giant figure filling the doorway as if to block our escape. There's a sinister look of hatred in Richard's rage-filled eyes. Nora clings onto me tight – *too* tight – as she trembles in my arms at the sight of her husband.

'Go on,' he yells. 'Finish what you were saying.'

The challenge is right there, but Nora is a smart woman. She keeps her mouth shut just as any petrified victim would do. That's why I hold her so close, protecting her from more harm while I gaze up at Richard with my heart pounding. It's no secret what's about to happen.

So I do my best to protect her.

THE ROOM IS SO STILL you could hear a pin drop.

Richard lunges forward, then stops himself just a few feet from us.

'Yeah,' he says. 'That's what I thought.'

The next thing I do – and I don't know why I do it – is pull away from Nora, gently putting her hands back in her lap, then stand between her and Richard. My legs are so unsteady I could fall at any minute, but regardless, I take the high ground.

'You need to take a timeout,' I tell him, looking him dead in the eye. I wonder if he can see how scared I am because he doesn't so much as blink at my instruction. It's like he knows how fake my confidence is. 'I'm not kidding. Don't lay a hand on her.'

'I'm only going to say this once.' Richard steps around me, taking advantage of my inability to move. Before I know it, he's towering over Nora, who is now sobbing into her palms. 'Get out.'

His eyes don't leave me. He's staring into my soul as if to challenge me. Maybe I'm weak after all because I turn my head to look out the nearest window. The first thing I see is the sun shining through the snow. Is it just me, or is it melting a little? I could have sworn the snow surface was a few inches higher just yesterday.

It could mean we have a chance of escape, which faces me with two options: stand here now and fight a battle that's impossible to win, or step away long enough for the snow to melt and hope nothing bad happens between now and the moment I leave.

I look at Nora, who's now lowering her shaky hands. She nods at me as if to give her approval – as if she knows exactly what I'm thinking and is telling me it's okay. I can't quite bring myself to leave the room, even though Richard isn't offering much of a choice.

'Scream if you need me,' I tell her. 'Scream at the top of your lungs.'

Nora nods. My stomach drops, shame washing over me as I turn and leave the room. Disregarding every little warning bell my body is ringing, I turn my back on the bedroom. Richard's voice booms through the walls, shouting at her for gossiping, and I'm not surprised he's angry – if I were a misogynistic woman beater, I would want to keep it a secret, too. But now his secret is officially out, and I've seen it with my own two eyes.

As for me? All I can do is return to Jacob.

And make sure he doesn't get caught up in all this.

Chapter Thirteen

I'M amazed to see Nora moving freely around the house just a couple of hours later. She passes Jacob's open bedroom door in the middle of a session, he asks what happened to her face, and she tells him she had a little accident before storming off. To be fair, she's actually done an amazing job at hiding the bruise with makeup. But no amount of blender can disguise that swelling. She looks like she's gone the distance with Rocky Balboa.

At the end of the workday, Jacob heads to one of the living rooms to watch TV, clutching his book to his chest. I can see he's near the end, and it seems he's doing what I always did when I was a kid – savouring the last few pages because it's too hard to say goodbye.

At least he's occupied. Staying out of his father's way can never be a bad thing. That leaves me alone to find Nora and check that she's okay. But before I do anything, I take one last look out the window and see the snow is picking back up again. Is it worth me trying to make the journey now? Will the extreme weather get better or worse overnight?

There's no way to tell for sure.

Nora is standing by the back door, staring out at the setting sun with her arms crossed. We can see each other's reflections in the door's glass pane, but she doesn't turn to look at me. Maybe she's embarrassed about her face. Not that she has anything to be ashamed of.

It's her pig husband who's to blame.

'Are you okay?' I ask, lowering my voice so Richard doesn't overhear.

'I'm fine. Thank you for patching me up.'

'I wouldn't be a very good person if I ignored it. Anyway, I feel really bad for leaving you alone with him.' This is truer than you can imagine – I've spent the whole day feeling like the worst person on Earth, almost as if running back to Jacob was a subconscious excuse to get out of the firing line. I'll never forget this overwhelming emotion.

'You did the right thing,' Nora says. 'He just needed to calm down.'

'But what about you? Did he hurt you again?'

'No, he just shouted a little.'

I nod approvingly, as if it's a good thing. It's not – it's just the lesser of two evils. After a few seconds of peace, I double-check we're alone and then go to stand right behind her, gazing out at the orange hue of the sky as it spreads a gorgeous palette across the settled snow. It'll be dark soon, which means the temperature will drop, and the swaying branches on the trees suggest there's already a pretty strong wind.

'I'm going to risk it,' I confess. 'I'm going to try getting help.'

Nora turns on the spot, her swelling having grown worse over the past couple of hours. She's staring at me with the wide eyes of a crack addict, shaking her head rapidly from side to side. 'No,' she says. 'No, you can't. You mustn't. Richard will—'

'Hit the roof?' I sigh. 'Yes, but I'll be back with the police by then.'

'How? He'll notice you've gone.'

'Not if I leave overnight.'

'It'll be even colder then. And the darkness, and the ground...'

Nora glances out the window. I can see something in her eyes. Hope, maybe. She wants me to try, but only if I succeed. She's trying to figure out if it's worth the risk, and I assure her it is. Worst-case scenario, I get caught in the snow and don't make it to town. Nora and Jacob will still be stuck up here with Richard, but at least she can pretend she didn't know I was leaving. That's *worst* case.

'Well?' I say as if seeking her permission.

Finally, she turns back to me and takes my hands. There's an undeniable chemistry between us – a sisterhood or some kind of caring, parental figure from me to her – and I feel like we could be good friends soon enough.

If only she would let me go.

'Dress up warm,' she says at long last. 'It's freezing out there.'

I TOOK NORA'S ADVICE: two thin jackets to go under my own large coat and a scarf with matching gloves that I took right from the downstairs cloakroom. She did offer me to take more, but I want to actually be able to move once I get outside.

After dinner – which I eat alone once again, of course – I retire to my room with the door open. As

I'm at the end of the hall, it's very unlikely anyone is going to pass and catch me watching the door, but at least this way, I can keep my eyes and ears open and know for certain when everyone has gone to bed.

Only then will I attempt escape.

The snow is billowing against the window, having picked up as soon as night fell. The world looks white out there – bright. Optimistic, even. But it's easy to say that from the warm comfort of a bedroom, where the heating is on and I'm wearing multiple layers. When I get out there, high up on a hill where the arctic wind is at its fiercest, it's going to hit me way harder than I can even begin to imagine.

But it's worth it.

If only to save this family.

It's a little after ten when the hallway light goes off. I swallow with great difficulty. It's like swallowing a LEGO brick. My anxiety about the weather is starting to peak. This is the moment, I realise, when things are either going to go really well or really poorly.

But at least I'm prepared.

I wait an extra few minutes to make sure everyone has time to get into bed, then creep downstairs in the dark. When I reach the back door (it's furthest away from Richard's bedroom, so there's less chance of him hearing me leave), I don the gloves and two hats, then step outside.

The cold hits me immediately. The breath is sucked out of me, and I gasp. For just a moment, I think about aborting the mission and running back inside to my comfort zone, but then I remember Nora's face – the sheer terror she has for her own husband.

And little Jacob, who could just as easily be next.

No, I have to do this. I try to relax my stiff muscles, close the door before the wind slams it shut, then make my way towards the woods at the back of the garden. From my bedroom window, I managed to see that the wall ends where the trees begin, and if I risk taking a stroll through the woods, then I can make it around the wall and start gaining some distance from this fortress. It sounds easy, but it certainly won't be.

My toes are already numb by the time I leave the garden. The snow is slightly thinner between the trees – the branches are holding a lot of it – but I must be careful. The ground is uneven, and steep banks appear on either side. Taking the long way, I grab hold of tree trunks for support and pass by as slowly as possible, careful not to lose my footing.

It feels like hours before I make it around the wall, but it's probably only been a matter of minutes. I stand still to catch my breath, looking back at the house one more time. Should I be alarmed that one of the lights is on? I think it's the hallway, though I'm unsure. Hopefully, nobody notices I'm gone.

Especially Richard.

I persevere, the biting wind gusting between the trees and gnawing at my cheeks. I can't feel my face, my feet are starting to burn with cold – yes, actually *burn* – and even my gloved fingers are losing some flexibility. It's best to make use of them before they're totally useless.

So far, so good, I think as I manoeuvre through the trees. It's not far now until I'm out of the woods. What will I even do when I get out? It will be a long and dangerous trip down the hill, which I'm not sure I could handle even if I didn't have to go through the wooded obstacle course first. I guess I should find the gate that runs up the main road so I can hold it for support.

But would that be enough?

What about when I get into town?

The town has probably gone to sleep by now, so I'll have to bang on a few doors. Maybe find a police station if there is one, quickly giving them the whole story of what's been happening to Nora. I hope they act on it – they should, considering a young child's safety is at risk. Although there's no telling how quickly they'll respond to such a thing.

Immediately, I hope. Anything could happen really, seeing as I managed to make it this far in such extreme conditions. I smile and laugh aloud when I realise how lucky I am, then continue through the icy terrain as cautiously as possible.

My luck ends when I find a steep bank. My foot slides out from under me, a torrent of snow rushing to the lower ground. I let out a scream as I fall, but the wind shoves it right back down my throat. I hit the dirt with a thud, pain shooting up my back. I wish that was it, but a branch catches my coat, and I spin. Fear fires through every inch of my body as I plummet towards the bottom of a bank at frightening speed.

I don't see the rock at the bottom until it's too late.

. . .

THE SNOW COVERS me within minutes... or has it been hours? It's too hard to tell since I've been diving in and out of consciousness for some time. My skull is alive with agony after hitting the rock. Even in the dark, I can see the blood that's trickled from my head and glazed the snow, like cherry syrup on a slushie.

Pain this intense is new to me. It's not just the wound or the bashing my body took as I fell, but the cold is also setting in. Even if I look past the pain, the fear is driving me crazy. I'm too exhausted to move and unable to do so even if I wasn't.

To tell the truth, I just might die out here.

I black out again, waking up God knows how much later. Things are getting a little foggy, and the snow flurrying directly into my eyes isn't helping. I squint, trying to hold up an arm and shield my face but quickly finding my strength has left me. This is it, I realise now.

This is where my story ends.

But it can't. Not now. Not when Nora is still back in the house. Or is she? I'm almost sure it's a hallucination, but I see her stomping through the snow, that same hunched-over, bashful woman dragging her feet through the thick blanket towards me.

Yeah, this is it, I think. *She's coming to save me.*

It's not until she's standing over me that I fully understand it's a hallucination. Because the figure I'm seeing in the dead of this ice-cold night is not Nora at all. It's Richard, and he's bending over to check my wound. "The Good Doctor" seems almost funny now.

'You can't die out here,' he says. 'Let's get you inside.'

Still unsure if this is real or not, I let him lift me while dwelling on his words. Of course he doesn't want me to die out here where everyone can see. He probably wants to finish me off in the house, then abandon my lifeless corpse in the same place as Katie's. Is this a new routine for him now? To bury a bunch of private tutors in one spot?

God help him if we're ever found.

Somehow, Richard manages to pick me up. Even with the weather fighting against him, he carries me in his strong arms and stomps through the snow. My eyes are closing as his body heat warms me, and I slip into a deep sleep that could easily just be death. If this is how I'm going to die – imagining body heat that simply isn't there – it's not the worst way to go.

Because at least I'm not alone.

Chapter Fourteen

You know in films when the hero will suddenly shoot awake, sitting up dramatically and walking around in the room? Well, I'm here to officially tell you that is so untrue it might as well have been told to you by a politician.

What really happens is that I start to dream. It's nothing big – just a core memory of when I fell over on the school playground and the teacher helped pick me up. My eyes start to slowly open, like they weigh a ton as my mind connects the dots between the playground incident and my tumble out in the snow. I don't even have the energy to lift my head, so I'm stuck squinting at a white ceiling. I'd mistake this place for Heaven if my skull wasn't throbbing so hard.

'I suggest not moving,' comes a deep voice from my side.

Honestly, if I didn't feel like I'd been hit by a lorry, I would spin around and try to see who it is. It's just as well that I know the voice all too well. I've heard that sternness before – the seriousness in his tone as he makes his threat.

Richard has me.

I try to speak, but words fail me. My mouth opens just enough to try forcing something out – questions, so many questions – but then something hard strikes me on the head. I hiss at the sting, the pain kissing my skin so hard I want to scream and leap to my feet.

As if he would let me.

'I know it hurts,' he says, though I still can't see his face. 'But it's just an alcohol swab. It will do you the world of good if you can just deal with the shock.'

An alcohol swab? Why on earth is he...?

Then I remember. The miniature avalanche beneath me. The beating my body took as I fell and the rock I hurtled towards so fast it knocked me out. I vaguely recall falling in and out of sleep, panicking as the night air threatened to freeze me to death. Then a figure appeared in the night, scooping me into his strong arms and...

Richard... saved me?

'Why are you helping me?' I manage to ask.

'Because I'm a doctor. It's what we do.'

'But you're...'

'A bad person. Yes, I know.'

I don't say anything because my life is in his hands. However, as the seconds tick by, I suddenly find myself able to rotate my head a little. I look around the room at the décor – it's all polished oak and marble. There's a wide, expensive desk that looks like it belongs in a study hall, a bookshelf that's packed to the brim with an assortment of colours, and – sitting on a wall rack high above the desk chair – a rifle. I know nothing at all about guns, but I'm smart enough to know they're dangerous in the wrong hands.

Richard must sense something in my reaction because he takes a break from dabbing my forehead to look at the gun. 'It's a vintage double rifle. Holds two rounds, and it's worth a little over a quarter million. It was my father's.' He turns back to me and stares, then: 'For display purposes only. That's a hunter's gun, and I don't hunt.'

I nod softly because it's all I can do. To be

honest, I believe him. Just because he hits his wife around and doesn't know how to be polite to his son's tutor, it doesn't mean he's a killer. It makes me wonder if I've blown this whole thing out of proportion. This whole time, I've been thinking he murdered her and buried her out in the woods.

But he saved *me*.

'Why are you helping me?' I ask again.

'I told you, I'm a doctor.'

'Yes, but I was leaving so I could report your abuse.'

'Obviously, I don't blame you for that, but I didn't want it to happen.'

'But you'll have to let me go at some point.'

'I know that.'

'And Nora? Is she okay?'

Richard shrugs like it's none of his business, packs the used cotton balls into a plastic bag, and then folds it up. Rather than pay attention to answering me, he takes a blanket off a nearby shelf and drops it onto me, leaving me to unfold it.

'I saw you leaving,' he says, 'and had to stop you. That's all.'

'You're not going to... kill me, are you?'

'If you need to die, it will happen when it happens. Until then, get some rest.'

With that, he turns on his heel and leaves me alone in his office. I won't lie – his final words leave me feeling even colder than I was outside. I have half a mind to grab that rifle from the wall and use it to take him down before he does the same to me. It's true that he saved me, but he said himself that he had to stop me from leaving. If I had to guess, I'd say he only saved me to keep himself squeaky clean when the police next come knocking.

And if I ever get out of here, they *will* come.

I'll make sure of it.

After a whole day on that office sofa, I'm starting to feel a little better. The feeling has returned to my body, so I'm able to walk up and down the length of the office while eyeing that rifle. It's terrifying to know that I may need to use it soon.

Despite how he normally treats women, Richard has left me a tray of food to consume over a long period of time (this is to keep him from having to pay frequent visits while he takes his work laptop to a different room) and a large pitcher of water I'm trying not to drink in one gulp. It's all gone before the sun even goes down again.

I'm just settling in to sleep when a weak knock hits the door. No sooner does the second tap sound than the door opens, and Nora pokes her head through the gap. She looks like a little mouse, too afraid to come in because she might get trampled on.

She should know by now that I'm not the one who hurts her.

'I've been told to send you back to your own room,' she says, slowly edging her way inside. Nora looks around the room as she comes to my side, as if she either hasn't been in here for a while or has *never* seen this side of the door. 'How are you feeling?'

'A bit better.'

'At least our faces match now.'

Considering how battered she looks, this inflicts panic. 'Is it that bad?'

'No, I was joking.' Nora smiles thinly. 'Sorry you didn't make it into town.'

'I'm the one who should be sorry. Looks like we're still stuck here.'

'Richard did... save you.'

I nod, slowly getting up from the sofa and folding up the blanket. Manners are manners. 'That's true. It actually got me thinking that maybe he's not the worst person in the world. If we just do as he says until the snow melts, maybe we can...'

Nora shaking her head is what stops me. There's hopelessness in her eyes, as if she's ready to fully give up. 'No, see, this is what he does. He lures you into thinking he's a decent man. That's how he got me, and that's how he got Katie. Maybe you're somewhat right – his heart might be in a good place – but it's the outbursts he has trouble controlling. So of course he saved you, but that doesn't mean he won't hurt you.'

'I could talk to him about the hitting if you like?'

'Please, Emma. Don't upset him. I don't want you to suffer like she did.'

My blood runs cold all over again. It's like I'm back out in the snow. I study her bruised face and want to ask about Katie. What was it she did that was so bad? What did Richard do to her and why? There's only one way to find out.

'Nora—'

'I've already said too much. Just... don't trust him, okay?'

Our eyes meet, and I see my frightened little friend all over again. Of course I don't want to end up like her, so I know better than to go poking around in Richard's business. From now on, I'll keep myself to myself until I'm fully ready to leave.

'All right,' I tell her. 'But I expect answers about Katie someday.'

'When the time is right, you'll get them.'

Nora leaves without me, and I take a few minutes before standing up.

Looks like the pain hasn't fully subsided after all.

I'm settled back in my room just a few minutes later. My head is pounding, and I'm feeling groggy, but otherwise, I'm going to come out of this okay. The biggest surprise is not that Richard helped me – it's more than clear that he just did it to keep his nose clean – but that I have stitches in my forehead from that goddamn rock.

I touch them softly, feel the sting, then return my hand to my armpit and squeeze myself while gazing out at the town of Wedchester. The snow is definitely thinning. So much, in fact, that I might make it out of here within just a couple of days. It makes me wish I had waited before venturing off into the woods. Maybe then I wouldn't have stitches.

Maybe then I wouldn't be tortured with the knowledge that there's a rifle in the house.

However, I do feel a little closer to Richard. It's an uncomfortable closeness that leaves me feeling colder than the icy winds outside, but what's that famous saying? Keep your friends close and your enemies closer? I never was one for sucking up to people, but I'll make the effort to stay in Richard's good books until it's time to leave.

I'll start by thanking him for fishing me out of the snow. As soon as I'm able to walk without the support of the banister, I head down the hallway and the stairs, then go right for his office on the ground floor. The door is shut – unlike how I left it – so he must be in there.

I knock, then wait with my hands stuffed in my pockets.

After a while, Richard pulls open the door and gawks down at me. The most disturbing thing about his appearance is that he's transformed back into the man who can't bear to look at me. His lips are threatening to sneer, disgust riddling his expression while he waits impatiently for me to explain the reason for this interruption.

'What?' he says after a long wait.

'I just...' Any courage I had upstairs is now

gone. Honestly, I thought I'd be talking to a warmer, more friendly version of Richard. Perhaps the man that saved me and took the time to patch me up. 'I just wanted to thank you for what you did.'

Richard stares right into my eyes, making me hold my breath.

It takes a while to realise he's staring at my forehead.

'Ask Nora for some antiseptic cream. You'll want to keep that germ-free.'

'Oh, I will.'

'How are you feeling?'

'Okay, I guess. A little fatigued.'

'Then get some rest. You're back to work tomorrow.'

The door bangs shut in my face, my hair brushing backwards at the force of the slam. I step back, my mouth hung open in shock. Okay, I shouldn't be too surprised that the man responsible for Katie's disappearance was rude to me, but I thought we'd turned a corner.

Obviously not.

There's a weird feeling settling in my stomach now. As I head back upstairs to crawl into bed and sleep off some of the pain, I hear Nora and Jacob playing in one of the rooms. It's nice to hear them interacting for once, but how long will this peace last? If Richard knows I'll be going home soon, he must be starting to sweat about what I'll tell people. Desperation can do funny things to a man, and that is exactly what makes me realise what this stomach pain is.

It's fear.

Chapter Fifteen

I AWAKE two days later to an amazing surprise.

Although I was initially sleepy and grumpy, I roll out of bed and rip open the curtains to find the sun shining down on Wedchester. The town has come to life again, the snow thawed and life returning to normal. The people look so happy from up here, and I don't know if it's the sunshine or the fact I'll get to leave, but suddenly, my spirits are lifted.

That's right – I get to *leave*.

I need to run it by my employers, of course. Well, they're more than that and even much more than my landlords, but Nora has become something of a friend over time. An outsider looking in might say that I've done more for her than she has for me, but the very fact I have a roof over my head begs to differ. Since being snowed in, I've been housed and fed. Not only has this family provided that for free, but they're still paying me for being here.

It doesn't get any better than this.

If you ignore the domestic abuse, that is.

In my own merry little way, I take a shower and avoid letting the spray hit my wounded forehead. As soon as I'm done, I throw on some clean clothes – a pair of jeans with a T-shirt and a zip-up hoodie in case I get cold – then head downstairs for breakfast.

Nora is in the hallway with a dust cloth, wiping down the grandfather clock. Behind her, the door to the kitchen is wide open, and a beam of light bleeds into the hall. A smell is emanating from that room, too, which Nora is quick to address.

'I cooked breakfast a little early this morning,' she says without looking up. 'Help yourself to anything you want, but save some for Richard. I think you'll find the quantity more than sufficient, so no need to be reserved if you have an appetite.'

I thank her, a little too focused on how eager she is to please. *Anything* she does for me is *more* than sufficient. I really want her to see that she doesn't owe me anything. Neither does she owe Richard, as a dutiful housewife or otherwise.

'The snow is melting,' I tell her excitedly.

'Yes, I noticed that.'

'Would you mind if I leave tonight?'

Nora puts down the duster and blows a stray blonde hair away from her face. 'It's not up to me what you do. If you think you can make it back into town safely, then be my guest. Would you like me to call you a taxi and have it ready for when you finish work?'

'I doubt they'll be operating so soon. The roads must still be icy. But thank you.'

'Well, if there's anything else you need, then just let me know.'

'Actually...' I step a little closer and lower my voice. 'We should focus more on what to do when I get down there. You've mentioned how uncomfortable you feel about me calling the police, and I won't do anything without your permission, but I would encourage it.'

Nora looks down thoughtfully. She knows the weight of this decision – that it will tear her family apart, even if she does come out of it safely. However Richard reacts, reporting him to the authorities is guaranteed to drive a wedge between them.

That's putting it lightly.

'I don't know what to do,' she confesses. 'What if he hurts me again?'

'That's the whole point. We can avoid it.'

'But if he hears sirens coming up the hill…'

'I'll tell them to be discreet.'

Nora pauses again, considering her options. I'll never truly understand why she keeps defending her husband, but isn't that a part of marital abuse? For the authoritarian to keep the weaker party on their side? It's controlling and manipulative.

And it seems to work.

'Can I have a think about it and let you know?' she asks, picking the duster back up.

'Of course you can.' I give her my warmest smile. 'We have all day.'

I head into the kitchen and keep an eye on the weather outside while filling my plate. The air is clear, and the sun is shining, so there are no signs of getting snowed in again. This is it – my day to get out of here and return to the bed and breakfast, away from all the danger.

As for Nora… we'll see.

. . .

It's starting to feel so natural having Jacob with me.

Even if it does feel temporary.

His education is coming along incredibly well, and I'm so proud of him. In fact, he barely feels like the same kid I met only a few days ago. Now that he's out of his shell, there's a youthful vibrance to him that sparks to life every time I'm around him. This is the importance of finding joy in our lessons – now he truly enjoys them.

'I hope you're feeling better,' he says as I sit beside him.

The kind comment takes me by surprise. Not because of his interest in the matter, but because of how much he knows. I was under the impression his parents hadn't told him anything – it was decidedly best for him to not know that I was trying to escape the Evil Mansion of Doom. That alone would open up a lot of questions.

'How do you know I hurt myself?' I ask.

Jacob scratches his pudgy little cheek. 'The back door is under my room. I heard you leave and watched out the window when you left. Then I saw Daddy bring you back a while later. I hope you didn't get too hurt.'

I smile kindly at him, wondering if it was truly

just a few minutes between me entering the woods and being carried back by Richard. Falling unconscious every five seconds does something to a person's sense of time. Just like everything else lately.

'I was really worried about you,' Jacob says, putting down his pencil.

'Aww. You were?'

'Yeah. I thought you weren't coming back.'

'Why would you think that?'

'Because Katie did the same thing.'

My body flushes with cold. One more mention of Katie and I'm going to go mad. It's horrible how alluring this mystery is, but the way I see it, it's directly connected to my chance of leaving this house alive... isn't it?

'What did Katie do?' I ask.

Jacob half-heartedly points at the window. 'She went for a walk.'

'Into the woods?'

'Yeah.'

'And you never saw her again?'

'Nope. Daddy went after her, too.'

'Just like with me? A few minutes later?'

Jacob nods, puffs out a sigh, then goes back to his book. With a comment like that, how could I possibly ignore the disappearance of his last tutor? Katie goes walking into the night, and Richard heads after her... so is she still out there? Did he bury her out there?

My head is a stir of thoughts: Jacob's grave drawing, Richard's temper, Nora's bruises, and the little I know about the police's investigation on the matter. If I'm going to leave this house tonight, there's one thing I'm absolutely not going to leave without.

The truth about Katie's whereabouts.

First things first: Jacob needs a distraction long enough for me to get what I need. This is easily done by promising him he can take a break from schooling and just lay down to read. He's finished his last book and is excited by the prospect of starting another, so that's taken care of.

Next, I check Richard is in his office and won't interrupt us. I've made my mind up to demand answers from Nora, no matter how hard it is for her. The last thing we need is for her husband to walk in and derail the conversation.

I find Nora in the dining room, Elvis Presley singing gently from the nearby vinyl player while she puts together a jigsaw puzzle. There's a glass of wine at her side, which I try not to judge her for –

it may only be ten o'clock in the morning, but she's been having a hard life for some time now. She looks up as I enter.

'Calm down. It's just grape juice,' she says with a forced smile.

I don't return the smile because I simply don't feel like it. This job has been wearing me down since the very beginning, and it's not even because of the work itself. I invite myself into the room, drag out a chair, and sit at her side.

'It's time we talk about Katie,' I say matter-of-factly.

Nora eyes me suspiciously, almost like she can't quite believe the nerve I've suddenly summoned. It's not that surprising when you consider how good my manners usually are, but it's also important to remember Nora is a victim of domestic abuse – being forceful with her is guaranteed to go in one extreme direction or another.

'What about her?' she asks.

'You know what happened to her.'

'It's not that simple.'

'You *know* what happened to her,' I say again, standing my ground.

Nora lowers her eyes to her puzzle, takes a sip of the grape juice that I now get a fruity whiff of, then sets it down. When she's done, she still doesn't look at me. This is really hard for her, I understand that, but it doesn't mean I shouldn't know.

'Richard will kill me,' she says.

'Why? Is that what he did to Katie?'

'Please, Emma—'

'No, I deserve answers.' I grab the seat of my chair and pull myself closer to her. Nora shrinks as I close the distance between us. It swathes me in guilt, but this is the only way to get the truth out of her, and it's better now than when it's too late. 'I know this is hard, but someone went missing up on this hill. That's someone's daughter. Someone's friend. There are people out there wondering where she is, and you're the only thing standing in the way of their closure. Don't you want them to know peace?'

Nora's eyes begin to sparkle with the early signs of tears. Her hands have started shaking, so she clasps them together and watches them. I'm close to making her talk – I can feel it – I just need to lean on her a little harder before she can talk herself out of it.

'Nobody has to know you told me,' I assure her. 'Whatever I learn, I'll just pretend I found it out by myself or lie and say I was going through Richard's things. But I know something happened to her, and I know Richard is behind it. You just need to clarify some things and let me in. Then, and only then, can we decide whether to report it. Together.'

She looks up at that last word, looking me dead in the eye. There's trust in there, possibly even some hope, but she keeps those thoughts to herself while she scrapes her chair back and goes to the window, her back to me as she looks out at the massive, green-white garden.

'You'll tell the police,' she says.

'Only if you permit me.'

'No. When you hear the truth, you'll tell them.'

I don't know what exactly she has to confess, but I have a pretty good idea. All I've been looking for is some kind of confirmation that Katie is dead. Proof, even, if there is such a thing. That's how the story would end: Richard being arrested and Nora finding a new home for her and Jacob. Hell, they could even keep this one, depending on their situation.

'Promise me,' Nora says. 'Promise me that if I tell you the truth, you won't tell the police until I've given the go-ahead. No matter how bad it is, you need to refrain until I'm ready for people to find out. Can you give me your word?'

I've said before that a promise is everything to me, so I don't take a request like this lightly. But if that's what it'll take to know the truth once and for all, there's not really any choice. It's time to finally unravel the mystery.

'Okay,' I say. 'I promise. Now, tell me everything.'

Chapter Sixteen

'Close the door,' Nora says, nodding towards it.

My mouth has gone dry in eager anticipation of learning the truth. I rush for the door, check the hall for signs of Richard, and, satisfied, push it to a close. Alone now, I go to the window and stand beside Nora, looking out at the garden together.

'To understand what happened with Katie, you first need to know a little bit about her,' Nora says. 'You see, she was a very bright and bubbly person. The type who everyone warms to the second she enters the room. All three of us – Richard, Jacob, and myself – were enamoured by her from the very first moment we met. It helped that she did a wonderful job with my son's education, too.

'She also had an insatiable appetite for knowledge. Not just in the academic sense either, but she took a sudden interest in Richard's work. You've probably realised by now that Richard is very private about his career. I mean, he doesn't even tell me about what happens throughout his workday. Never did. Apparently, he's been in trouble for it in the past.'

I hug my arms around my chest. 'For sharing details of his work?'

'Well, not quite. There was an incident many years ago – long before we met – where he had sex with a patient in his office at the surgery. It was consensual in nature and occurred more than once, but eventually, it had to come to an end. It was Richard who broke it off, explaining that he needed to focus on himself for a little while.

'But his patient didn't like that too much, so she reported him to his superiors. As you can imagine, it kept him from practising for some time as he was being investigated. While this was going on, he found that his only defence was to have some firm words with her and insist that she stop. Let's just say she did not take it well.'

I shake my head, grind my teeth from side to side. This conversation is already making me uncomfortable, but it's something I need to hear. I remain quiet and let Nora continue.

'She saw it coming and had her phone recording, ready to destroy his career and his entire life in the process. Thankfully, she was stupid enough to reveal this to him then and there, so he took her phone to protect himself, then left and put it in his office drawer. Later, somebody sneaked in and took that phone, using it as incriminating evidence against him.

'At least, that's what they wanted to do. Richard was smart enough to delete the video before it went back into that woman's hands, so she had nothing to bargain with. After a long, thorough investigation – Richard denying ever having slept with her, I might add – he returned to work and never heard from her again. She took her own life a few months later.'

'God.' I raise a hand to my mouth.

'God doesn't take lives. That's the Devil's job.' Nora clears her throat. 'But this isn't about the patient. This is all to help you understand why Richard is so private. He absolutely refuses to talk about anything to do with work, and there's nothing he hates more than having people in his office without his approval. This is why he works from home, too – no people to see, no risk of being accused of things. Do you see what I mean?'

I nod. 'Yes, but what does this have to do with Katie?'

'Well, like I said, Katie was very interested in his work. I honestly believe it was innocent – she was just a curious person by nature – and one day made the mistake of snooping around his office. I don't know what she could possibly have said to upset him further, but I heard Richard screaming even from upstairs, even throwing something that shattered. I did go downstairs to investigate, or... I started to, but then I saw her running out of the house and into the woods at the back of the garden. That's how defensive he got over his personal space, and it's been the same ever since. That's why I never go into his office.

'It's probably not that surprising to learn I was curious, so I stood there and watched for a long time. First, Richard ran after her and followed her into the trees. I thought that was it and that they'd soon come back and figure things out between them. But...'

Nora starts biting her nails, her hand shaking like an autumn leaf.

'Go on,' I tell her, my stomach churning at the thought of Katie's murder.

'No.' Nora shakes her head and wipes away a tear. 'You should come with me.'

'Where?'

'Upstairs.'

'What about the story?'

'Don't worry, you're not going to miss out on anything. It's just that you need to see this before I go any further.' Nora reaches out a hand, which I take, and I realise how cold it is when she leads me out of the room. 'Trust me. You'll want to see this.'

Nora pushes open one of the doors that has been closed ever since I got here. What I see is a bedroom almost identical to my own – just like how hotels would decorate their rooms the same – except there are some belongings in an open suitcase on the bed.

Nora goes to them.

'These belonged to Katie,' she says, touching them lightly. 'Come and see.'

I move forward and approach the bed, her phrasing not lost on me: *belonged* to Katie. Even though I'm slowly learning about the events leading up to her disappearance, it's like the ending has already been given away. But even more interesting than the 'what' is the 'how'. That's why I'm so intrigued by the contents of the suitcase.

'It's everything she had when she came to this house,' Nora says.

'The police didn't take it?'

'No. Richard hid it.'

My hands reach out to spread the things apart. It's nothing special: some clothes, a handful of expensive-looking jewellery, a laptop, and a bunch of paperwork that outlined her lessons with Jacob. A thought crosses my mind, but it rushes out of Nora's mouth first.

'This is the first thing that made me think she's dead,' she says. 'If Katie had a reason to run away and start a new life, she would have at least taken these things with her. Now, I know she was in a hurry, but wouldn't she come back for them later? With the police, perhaps?'

I nod along, almost feeling her presence as I touch her belongings. It's like a ghost has entered the room and is standing over me. That could be why I feel so cold. It's like someone just walked over my grave. Maybe they did.

'What's the second thing?' I ask.

Nora looks at me quizzically.

'You said this was the first thing that made you think she died. What's the second?'

'Ah. Yes.' Nora goes to the bedroom window and points. I step to her side and follow her finger. 'See that small opening in the trees there? That's where Richard came out. He was all red-faced like he'd been running a marathon, but his clothes were a mess. Almost as if there had been some sort of a tumble. I don't know anything about fighting, but Katie was no bigger than you are, and Richard... well, you've met him.'

I certainly have. He's not only big enough to hurt a small and fragile woman, but I know from experience he has the strength to pick one up and carry her through the snow. If Katie was truly around my size, the poor girl didn't stand a chance.

'I watched from this window for a while,' Nora goes on. 'Richard came back into the house, and I waited for Katie to do the same thing. Only she never did. What *did* happen, however, was Richard went back out into the woods with one of those thick sacks builders tend to use. I watched, waited, and then saw...'

Nora's voice goes weak, breaks, and then she starts to cry again.

I put a hand on her bony shoulder. 'What did you see, Nora?'

'It's... he came back half an hour later.'

'Back into the house?'

'No. Not to the house. He was hauling that sack around, except this time it was full.'

Sheer terror rips right through me. The image of Richard carrying a giant sack out of the woods makes my mouth go numb. It's useless trying to talk because all that will come out is a torrent of terrified whines. I'm not normally this pathetic, but the reality of the situation has me grounded – what am I supposed to do with this information?

Still crying, Nora wipes a tear and points again through the window. Shivering, I trace the direction of her finger to something else – something I didn't even think of until now.

'There,' she says. 'That's where he took the sack.'

Now I understand everything. What Katie did to upset Richard. *Why* it upset him so much and what he did to her out in those woods. Any big secret that can bring Nora to tears is sure to instil fear into my already breaking heart, but as I piece it all together and stare out at Katie's resting place, I finally understand why the police never found her body.

It's because she was down the well.

Is down the well, I remind myself.

That's when I start to cry, too.

I shouldn't do it, but I can't help myself.

Blame my unquenchable thirst for answers – my undying need to solve this mystery and move on with my life. Not without stopping by the police station and reporting it, that is. Providing Nora will let me. I wonder, could I break a promise if I find what I think I'll find? If I head out to the well right now?

There's only one way to find out.

I leave Nora in the bedroom and head outside, fear driving me to inspect Katie's final resting place. If I see a body at the bottom, there's no telling how I'll feel or what I'll do. The nervous anticipation alone is making me shake, and I'm not even out in the cold yet. The truth is I'm petrified of finding something that might hint towards my potential fate.

Another truth is I'm too young to die.

Outside, the wind is bitter, but the sun is warm. That's exactly how I'm feeling, too – conflicted. I feel for Nora, but I can't not report a death. I made a promise, but if there's a young woman's body at the bottom of the well, I have a duty as a human being to report it. Not only that, but Jacob and his mother will need to get pulled far away from Richard as fast as humanly possible. If not, they may suffer the same fate.

My heart is beating like a drum when I approach the well. I rest my hands on the cold brick and close my eyes. I suck in a deep breath and calm myself. My version of calm, anyway. It's not entirely possible to keep from panic in a situation like this.

When I feel as ready as I'll ever feel, I open my eyes and look down. It's dark at first, the well's roof keeping the sunlight from filling the hole. I lean over a little, squinting into the dark and seeing an outline or shape of... something? It could be water or rocks.

It could be a body.

Before I find out, something hits me. Two short, sharp jabs at the same time, right in my back. I lose my balance immediately, the air leaving my lungs in a soundless scream as my feet leave the ground. Brick scratches at my belly as I topple, skin tearing from my leg as I plummet into the well. I don't even see the hands that shoved me, and all I can think in those few seconds is that I'll never live to see my family again.

Then, in the bat of an eye, the ground rushes up to hit me.

And everything goes dark.

Chapter Seventeen

NORA

THE BITCH WAS ASKING TOO many questions.

She simply had to go.

To be honest, I never really thought it would get this far. Two private tutors within a year? That's the stuff mystery novels are made of, which simply isn't my genre. I was always more of a romantic type. That is, until Richard ruined our marriage. But we'll get to that.

First, I want to talk about what happened when Emma arrived on our doorstep. She came out of the blue, like lightning wanting to make its mark. I wasn't entirely upset to meet her either – Jacob needed his education just like any other child, and she seemed to fit the bill. Not only that, but she was pleasant enough to begin with. I sort of liked her... until I didn't.

That's another thing we'll get to.

On the day Emma started working in our house, I set her up in Jacob's bedroom and left her to it, then went about my household chores. There was plenty of cleaning to do, but I hurt myself early in the morning. It was Richard's fault, really – he always crammed the clothes into his drawers too tight, so the bottom sagged out and the clothes caught on the drawer above. I had to wrestle it open to put some new clothes in (I'll be damned if I will sort out this whole mess for him), then bang it shut. But I didn't account for the protruding drawer above, which my arm smacked into so hard I wanted to shout. The pain was explosive and deep, but I let it go and continued with my day just as intended. Everything was fine at that time.

The very next day, Emma happened to catch sight of the bruise on my arm. I saw the little look of concern she gave me, but I didn't want to say anything. She was probably very busy with Jacob, so the last thing she needed was to get caught up in my boring stories about Richard's underwear drawer and how I took a simple knock.

But she wouldn't leave it alone.

'What's this?' she asked, reaching out for my arm.

Naturally, I withdrew. 'It's nothing.'

'It's not *nothing*. It's as purple as Vimto.'

It was hard to believe an employee of mine would be so bold as to question me like that. To tell the truth, I took an instant dislike to her there and then, but it didn't register just yet. For now, I simply had to put her straight. 'This doesn't concern you.'

'I'm just one woman looking out for another. Let me see.'

With my sleeve rolled up, she examined the giant bruise and then looked at me with all the pity and sympathy in the world. An idea immediately fell into place. After what happened with Katie, would it really be the worst thing in the world to have Emma think I was being abused? The people in town believed it anyway, so what was one extra person?

The fact was the police were always going to come back again someday. Their trail would go cold before some new evidence would find its way to their desks, and then they'd start searching the grounds all over again. If that happened, it would be the end of me. I had to find a way to start pushing the blame onto my dear husband – if he took the fall, I could ride off into the sunset with my son at my side while Richard stayed locked behind bars for the rest of his life. It was amusing, really, because he wasn't the one to blame for Katie.

I was.

Kind of.

So I left with my cup of tea and let Emma make up her own mind on where that bruise came from. If one thing led to another, there was always the option of pointing the finger at my husband. All I had to do was cry from time to time, which was easy enough to do.

I just had to think about Katie.

Maybe it was a little arrogant of me to think I'd got away with it. Richard had always been very sneaky, and getting his daily steps in around the house was very important to him. The problem was, despite his size, I very rarely heard him coming.

Imagine my surprise when I saw him outside the room.

'You do realise I heard every word of that?' he said.

Look, nobody likes being caught out on a lie. Not that I *technically* lied – it was more like being silently ambiguous. There was time for that to change, of course, and I badly wanted it to. It'd been years since I truly loved Richard, so who cared what people thought of him?

'I'm not going to discuss this with you,' I said, breezing right past him.

Because he didn't want to be overheard shouting at me, he kept his voice low and followed me through the hall to my own private crafts room. I locked the door on him before he could get inside, shutting him out so I could enjoy my tea in peace. Even with him knocking on the door, I managed to enter a trance-like state as I stared out into our beautiful garden with my cup and saucer in hand. It always made me happy to view the grounds from up high.

Even if remembering what we'd done out there spoiled my good mood.

Eventually, the knocking stopped. Richard must have shuffled away because the next hour was one of the calmest, most soothing times I'd had in years. I sat in front of my art board and applied some thin brushstrokes to the paper, mixing together some greens and yellows to paint a perfect, summery field. It was my happy place, despite being tainted by the fact I had to leave that room at some point. And when I did, Richard would shout.

That's why I developed a plan to let Emma hear it.

With my nifty little idea in place, I finally left the craft room and stopped in the hallway that led to Richard's office. I called out to Jacob, just loud enough to make sure he couldn't hear me but Richard could. Clever, wasn't it?

Like a moth to the flame, the door swung open, and Richard came out to approach me once more. As soon as he laid eyes on me, I scoffed and walked down to the main hall, stopping halfway down the stairs where Emma must have been able to hear us. It was hard to hear anything in that enormous house, but if I could just get Richard to raise his voice…

'I want to know what you told Emily,' he spat, gripping my arm on the stairs.

'Emma,' I corrected him, glancing down at his hand.

He quickly removed it. 'Was it about Katie?'

'She knows enough to be curious, but nobody knows what happened to her.'

'So you didn't tell her the truth?'

'What are you talking about?'

'Don't play games with me, Nora. We're in enough trouble as it is.'

A small part of me enjoyed winding him up, but there was a purpose behind it. Katie's fate was always a sore subject around him, so it was guaranteed to make him raise his voice. All I had to do was grin and make one small comment to make him think I'd spilled the beans.

'Let's just say Emma knows what you're like,' I said.

Richard groaned, shook his head, and gritted his teeth as he began to shout. 'For the last time, I don't want you explaining the situation to the help. What happened to Katie is between you and me. If you're having trouble understanding that, then we're in some serious trouble.'

There. That was perfectly loud. If that wasn't enough to draw Emma's prying ears, nothing ever would be. Now that was in place, all I had to do was feel a little sorry for myself to provoke a tear. The pain would be heard in my voice, and – bingo

– Richard had an abused woman on his hands. It was too easy.

'I'm sorry,' I said, weeping. 'She asked me out of the blue, and—'

'Enough of the excuses, for crying out loud. And what about the bruise?'

'What about it?'

'Did you tell her the truth about where it came from?'

'No. I mean... of course I didn't, no.'

'Then what *did* you tell her?'

Our little conversation (performance) was interrupted by a sudden flurry of creaking floorboards that almost sounded like applause. Richard turned his head to listen, which gave me enough time to smear away my fake tear and smile. The son of a bitch was falling for all of it, and there wasn't a damn thing he could do to save himself.

'Is someone up there?' he yelled. 'Jacob? Emily?'

How many more times was he going to get her name wrong? Not that I minded too much – it all contributed to making him look like he didn't give a crap about her. Which was far from the truth. Richard was always kind to others, to his detriment, if I'm honest, but I'd put him in a situation where the more he said, the more words I was able to twist.

Moments later, he hurried up the stairs to check we weren't being spied on. That was the end for me. For that day, anyway. Emma had heard everything I'd wanted her to hear, and there was little more for Richard to say without just repeating himself.

It was ticking over nicely.

The weekend came and went quick enough, which gave me plenty of time to think. I pondered long and hard whether or not to lean on this whole abuse story, ultimately deciding it couldn't hurt. Richard had already seen signs of me manipulating people anyway, so it wasn't like it would shock him. Even if it did, what could he really do?

He knew I would take Jacob away from him if he stepped out of line.

Emma came to the door that morning, so chirpy it made me feel sick. I let her in as usual, but this time, I pulled her into the dusty old reading room none of us actually used. I deliberately chose that room because it was the furthest from

Richard's office, and I didn't want him overhearing the yarn I was about to spin.

'I've been thinking about what you asked me,' I told Emma. 'About my bruise.'

'Oh?'

'I'm not ready to tell you how it came to be, but would you do me a kindness?'

'Of course. What do you need?'

I dramatically looked over her shoulder, then took a few extra steps to lean out of the door and make sure nobody was around. When I returned to her, I took both her hands and looked her dead in the eye. 'It's really good to have you here. Not just so Jacob has a consistent tutor, but when you're here, Richard doesn't... I mean, he's...'

'Take your time,' Emma said soothingly, sounding a little condescending.

'Yes. I shouldn't...' I cleared my throat. 'I don't want you to leave. Not for a long time.'

I could see the shock on her face as she realised she had to stay. It was a question of morals: could she leave an abused housewife behind and move on to a new town? The truth was, I didn't want anything getting out. Jacob needed his education, and I wanted somebody who wasn't going to run to the next town and start blabbing about the things she saw and heard. So if only I could build a friendship with this woman…

'I'm not going anywhere,' she finally said. 'Is that the kindness you wanted from me?'

'Yes.' I nodded slowly. 'Please, promise me. No matter what—'

'S*now*!'

Jacob burst into the room then, blowing my plan to smithereens. It's not like I could blame him – I don't think he'd *ever* seen snow before, so he was bound to be a little hyped up. I just wished he hadn't thought to run in on us, blowing apart our conversation like some kind of energetic little wrecking ball. It was times like that I felt real spite towards him.

The rest of the communication had to be done with my eyes. I gave Emma my best puppy-dog expression. She stared at me for a long time, support and comfort beaming back at me without so much as a word. While Jacob darted between us on his way to the window, I got everything I needed from a short nod and a half-smile.

She wasn't going anywhere. I had her.

Hook, line, and sinker.

Chapter Eighteen

NORA

Things only got harder after Emma moved in with us; I had to cook for her, talk to her more often, and – most importantly of all – start watching what I said around her. Although she and Richard hadn't been in a room together since we got snowed in, it was all too easy for them to have a conversation and straighten everything out.

That was why I took the time to threaten my husband once again.

'Just so we're clear,' I told him while we lay in bed that night, a pillow between us as per usual. 'We're stuck in this situation together whether you like it or not. The difference is people will actually believe me if I say you killed Katie.'

I heard him huffing and puffing. 'Fuming' might even be the word. He sounded like some furnace deep in the bowels of an old house, groaning like he was about to roar, explode, or both. Before he could say anything, I reminded him why he should stay calm.

'Jacob may be our son, but that doesn't mean I can't hurt him.'

'Don't you dare threaten him,' Richard finally said, sitting up in bed.

'I don't *want* to, but I will if it helps you learn your place in this marriage.'

There wasn't one more word out of him that night, which was just as well. Of course, he had every opportunity to strangle me to death or hold a pillow over my face while I slept, but how would he get away with it now? Emma and the people of Wedchester knew (or thought) he had a violent streak, and I was the poor little abuse victim.

It was perfect.

The only thing that really caused me any problems was the fact he worked from home. He didn't want to, but ever since I started threatening Jacob, Richard insisted I couldn't be trusted around him.

That's why he was always in the house, and to be honest, I was sick of the sight of him. It was only getting harder each day, and he was still able to tell Emma the truth.

I had to double down and make her hate him even more.

After all, people usually believed the first side of the story they heard, right?

Call it an insurance policy if you like, but I quickly got the idea to stab myself with Richard's letter opener, wipe my prints and blood off it, then put it back. If push came to shove, the police could always find the blood with an ultraviolet light. Then, I made a deliberately bad job of patching it up, threw on a top that would easily show bleed-through, and carried on with my day, knowing Emma would see me way before Richard ever did.

The rest simply fell into place.

She found the blood on my sweatshirt while I was chopping vegetables in the kitchen. It caught her off guard, making her stumble as she gazed down at it in horror. The next words out of her mouth told me I'd already tricked her.

'Nora, did he hurt you?'

'Just leave it alone,' I said, crying in the performance of a lifetime.

'That's easier said than done.'

When she took the knife from my hand, I intensified the tears to fully win her over, then hesitantly met her request and showed her the wound. I could see the anger brewing in the depths of her eyes, jutting out her jaw as she saw undeniable (deniable) proof that I was being seriously harmed by my psychotic (sane) husband.

I gave her some cock and bull story about how I couldn't get dinner made on time. It was important that his reason for hurting me seemed silly and trivial, so what could be more trivial than taking too long to cook his dinner? Worst of all – for him, at least – he always had a habit of asking when dinner was so he could fit it around his schedule. It all added to making him look more guilty, and he didn't even know it was happening.

As long as I begged Emma not to confront him.

The problem was she had other ideas. She was trying to convince me that we should report it to the police. There was absolutely no way that was going to happen because the last thing we needed was to actually *invite* an investigation on our property. But it sort of worked in my favour, allowing me to lean into how scared I was of my own husband.

Then he came in, interrupting us.

While he stood there in the doorway demanding an explanation as to what he'd caught us talking about, I went as quiet as possible and let the rest take care of itself. Richard was an imposing character even when he didn't want to be, so of course, he looked scary in that moment. If the scene itself didn't sell it, my reaction to him being there did.

I'm telling you, I deserved an Oscar for that shit.

THE NEXT PIECE of evidence against Richard happened by accident. But before I explain, first I must tell you about what happened three years ago, back when I was pregnant a second time.

See, my parents were smokers. As were their parents, back in a time when nobody really knew how bad it was for you. Naturally, I took to the habit pretty early in my life. After the first few years of having it puffed into my face or having to sit in a room where all the adults were making the place look like there was heavy fog, I reached that early teen stage where everyone was trying it out.

We had to look cool, didn't we? Anyway, peer pressure was real.

Unlike most of my friends though, the addiction hit me really hard. My lungs were completely screwed by the time I was twenty-one. I tried quitting so many times over the years, but it never really stuck. The best I ever managed was to keep away from the disgusting (delicious) habit while I was pregnant with Jacob. The first thing I did after giving birth was to head outside and spark up. My daily intake of carbon monoxide skyrocketed after that, and there was no sign of it slowing down until I got pregnant once again.

Even then, it didn't stop right away. It's called an addiction for a reason, and I had it bad. Still, even with my heart doing flutters and my lungs feeling constantly tight, I couldn't keep my hands off them. I'd soon come to regret it.

Leah died of SIDS at only three months old – and yes, our children's names were deliberately biblical just to give us some sense of a higher power that might help us through our somewhat troubled marriage. Richard blamed me for her death, thanks to all the smoking. I didn't want to accept responsibility for that, but when I had a stroke that was caused by my addiction, it was time to fess up and quit for good.

But it wasn't for good.

I still smoked for a while, but it was more like once a day. This greatly increased my chance of a second stroke, but I didn't care. Still don't. The very best thing I had going on in my life was those five minutes or less it took to enjoy an entire cigarette. That wasn't going to change, no matter how bad things got.

This is all to say Richard *hated* it when I smoked.

I knew that, but it didn't stop me until he found out.

After leaving Emma out on the patio, I breezed right by him with hopes of getting away. He obviously smelled it all over my clothes, so he launched out a hand and grabbed my arm, stopping me in my tracks as he took a sniff at my hair.

'You've been smoking,' he said.

'Nope.' I sighed. 'You're just paranoid.'

'Nora, I can smell it all over you.'

You know those moments of panic where you're caught out on a lie? That was exactly what I was going through. The next thing out of my mouth was a quick fib to save myself from looking like the villain, telling him Emma was smoking and I was simply standing too close to her. This was actually one of the few instances in which Richard had a right to tell me what to do. I guess he just cared about my well-being, for whatever reason that was.

By the time Emma got back, we were almost at each other's throats. The sound of the door popping open made us both stop, turning towards her and staring like she was covered in something brown and sticky. I put on my best 'scared' face immediately.

'Do you have something to tell me?' Richard asked her.

It took a little probing, but Emma finally took the fall for me. I let out a breath of relief and tried not to smirk as he berated her for something she didn't even know not to do. How was she supposed to know my lungs were in trouble? She wasn't, and yet she took it like a champ. *Good little Emma*, I thought, and my self-satisfaction almost betrayed me.

'Not only do we have a young child in this house,' Richard stressed angrily, 'but I have a wife. Do you think I want her to walk around the house with your dirty cigarette smoke sunk into the fabric of her clothes? It stinks, Emma, and I don't like it.'

Emma went on to apologise profusely while Richard threw out my last pack of smokes – the bastard – before storming out. I rushed towards my saviour and threw my arms around her, thanking her for saving my life. Like I said earlier, this all happened by mistake, but I'm really glad it worked out so well. The evidence was mounting up against him, and all he'd really done that day was try to protect me.

More fool him.

The next morning, all of my plans backfired.

At least a little.

I was minding my own business, standing in the study room and letting my eyes roam around to pick out which bits I would change. We didn't often move rooms around, but I was getting sick of so many going unused. I know what you're thinking: how could a family of three make use of so many rooms in a house that size? Not well, but we tried our best: a gym, a games room, a cinema, a nursery, additional guest rooms, a room for collecting antiques, and even a sauna, among other things. There were a thousand things we could have done in that house, but Richard always complained that he was already worked to the bone and said there was no way we could ever afford all those changes. I didn't see why he couldn't have just worked more hours. Maybe he was just lazy.

My daydreaming was broken by the man himself, coming in to wreck my day. I'd barely turned around before he started barking at me, showing off a new-found confidence that would come back and bite him soon.

He just didn't know it yet.

'You know what?' he said, joining me at the oak desk. 'I've been thinking about how spoiled, cruel, and malicious you are. All those things you threatened to do? You go ahead and do them. Tell everyone your little stories about me, put your own little spin on the rare things that did actually happen, but I want you to know something.'

I turned around to look at him, somewhat alarmed about what he might have against me. I tried not to show it, and my acting had become pretty decent by that point, so it probably worked. I set my jaw and gave him a cold stare. 'What?'

'If I'm going down, I'm taking you with me.'

'Excuse me?'

'You heard.' Richard jabbed a pointed finger into my collarbone. I stepped back, anger flaring through my body. 'If you try spreading rumours that I hurt you, I'll tell the police you were in on the whole Katie thing. If you take Jacob away from me, I'll tell the police. If you so much as think about destroying our family, I'll—'

'Mum! Dad!' Jacob yelled, bursting into the room.

Our argument died as quickly as it had started. We both turned and stared at our son, who was bounding towards us like an excitable puppy. There was a book in his hand, but I barely took note of it because I was so wound up I could kill everyone in that room without remorse.

Needless to say, we didn't appreciate the interruption.

'This had better be important,' Richard said.

'It is.' Jacob ran over to us, book in hand. 'Look, I'm getting really good at reading!'

'That's really good, son, but now's not a good time.'

The look of disappointment on Jacob's face would have scared most mothers into giving up – dropping to their knees and imploring him to show off – but I was so pissed off it was taking all my strength to even look a little like I was scared to be near my husband. After all, Emma was standing by the door and watching.

I zoned out and missed the whole conversation between them, only coming back to that world once Emma left the room. Richard had timed his threats perfectly, but I couldn't just accept them and back down. If anything, I had to make more of an effort to ensure that Emma saw more – and I mean *tons* more – abuse from my dear husband.

It was a game he couldn't possibly win.

I hoped.

Chapter Nineteen

NORA

I could tell Richard was starting to sweat, otherwise he wouldn't have made those threats. I was rather confident he was bluffing, but it didn't hurt to bang myself around a bit, just in case. Well, it *did* hurt – it hurt like hell – but you know what I'm trying to say.

I told Richard I wasn't feeling well and tried to pass that lie by a qualified doctor. He offered to give me the once-over to make sure it was nothing serious, but I wasn't letting him near me. Fed up, he left the room and got to work.

Which gave me a chance to make some new bruises.

After spending some time gathering my courage in the bedroom, I threw myself around like a rag doll. I ran into open drawers, hurled myself off the bed, then realised I had to step up my game. These knocks were only leaving bruises under my clothing, but to take full control of Richard, I needed something bigger. Something severe.

I went into the bathroom to reduce the cleaning I'd have to do after. The door frame was solid oak, hard enough to break most bones if you hit it hard enough. I tried not to think too hard, grabbing both sides of it, closing my eyes, and then ramming my own face into the frame. Deep, agonising pain seared through my skull. There was a crunch in my nose, but thankfully, it only went numb. Blood rained down my chin and onto my clothes, then trickled onto the floor. I mopped that up while I still could, then took to the mirror to sort myself out.

My hands were shaking while I tried to fix this. Not just because of the fiery pain shooting through my face but because of the excitement to see where this would get me. Emma was dreadfully inquisitive, which would later be her downfall.

But be patient – you'll hear that part soon enough.

'Nora?' came a voice from outside. 'Are you in here?'

A wide grin spread across my face. My reflection in the mirror was bloody and maniacal, and I didn't much care for it. All the same, I had to force it away and go for the suffering-woman frown just for the sake of consistency.

Emma came in a moment later, first taking a small look and then gasping when she saw what I'd done to myself – what *Richard* had done, as I'd soon be telling her. I held the cotton balls in each hand, leaning over the basin as I gaped at her hopelessly in the mirror.

Then, for effect, I turned on the waterworks.

Predictable as ever, Emma ran into the room and started to treat my wounds while I filled her head with fiction about Richard. She listened, threatening to get help for me, which only made the anger inside me swell. *Throb*. Nonetheless, I continued selling her the idea that my husband had done this to me, taking it as far as possible.

Until he walked in on us.

'Go on,' Richard yelled, filling up the doorway. 'Finish what you were saying.'

To her credit, Emma actually tried standing up to him. It didn't get very far – mostly because I gave her the nod to leave the two of us alone – but her effort was commendable. The most urgent thing, however, was to separate her from Richard so I wouldn't have to speak in ambiguous dual languages. Who knew lying could be so hard?

As soon as she left the room, Richard started opening up, screaming in my face about how I shouldn't be gossiping. There was no way of telling how much he'd overheard, but it didn't matter. All I had to do was turn my back on him, brush my hair, and go about my day.

The rest would take care of itself.

LATER THAT SAME DAY, Emma revealed her plan to trek through the snow and get help in town. I didn't much care for her ambition to tear apart my family, but it was far too late to reveal the truth. After everything I'd done to frame Richard, the best I could do was play along and hope she didn't make it down to Wedchester.

Or I could make sure she didn't.

It was going to be hard work either way – the hill was steep, even if she got that far, and the woods were dangerous enough when it was raining. During a snow season, at night, when you couldn't see too far in front of you? It was unlikely she would survive.

Perhaps that's why I encouraged her.

Still, on the off-chance she might succeed on her journey, I waited until Richard and I were in bed before telling him. Emma must have already got to the trees by then, so she had a head start. Just enough to hurt herself, with any luck.

'What are you up to?' Richard asked from the bed as I rubbed lotion on my skin.

'Nothing. It's just that Emma was talking about going back to town.'

'You can't exactly blame her. It's hardly pleasant up here.'

'No, I mean tonight.'

Richard's head turned towards the window, where snow was raining against the glass so hard you could actually hear it. His face creased up with amazement and concern, the combination making him appear ten years older.

'Out there? Tonight?'

'That's what she said. Something about going through the woods.'

As quickly as that, he leapt out of bed and ran down the hall. I heard him yell her name (getting it right this time) before rushing back in to throw on some thick clothes. He snapped at me for 'just sitting there' while he went out to save our kid's tutor, but I didn't even pretend to care. I just smiled and picked up my paperback while he ventured outside.

I was hoping he'd find her dead, but he came back sometime later with Emma in his arms, taking her to the nearest room – his office, where all his medical supplies were – and shutting the door on me. It's hard to explain the hate I felt for Emma right then. Richard had never even let me into that room, so why should she be any different?

Richard was in and out, spanning overnight and the whole of the next day. I couldn't stop pacing around the house, telling Jacob to stay in his room while I just worried about what they were doing in there. It had occurred to me that my husband had the perfect opportunity to tell his side of the story – to convince our tutor that everything she knew about us was complete bull. I prayed my previous threats would make him keep his mouth shut.

But the only way to know was to ask her.

Richard had taken his laptop to a different room, so I used this to my advantage. As soon as I got the chance, I went into his office and told

Emma he wanted her out of there, back in her own bedroom, so he could continue with his job. Not only did this make him look more like he didn't give a damn about her, but it also separated the two. It was good thinking on my part, but I still couldn't help wondering how much she knew.

It was a good thing I spotted the rifle hanging on his office wall though.

If worse came to worst, I could always use that to ensure victory.

It should have been obvious that my lies were about to come out. Emma was getting too close, always nagging at me with questions about Katie and what was happening between Richard and me. I could only imagine what scenarios were playing out in her pretty little head.

All I knew was they were wrong.

The truth about Katie was something that would hopefully never come out. But if Emma made it back down that hill and started yapping about what she saw, people were going to start asking questions. I'd then be faced with having to continue the victim routine and implicating

Richard, and then it was only a matter of time before they discovered what had really happened.

And if his threats were real, he'd be taking me down with him.

Those were his words, not mine.

It only got worse after the incident with the en suite. I covered up my bruises with makeup and carried on with my life, letting events naturally take their course over time. Things actually started to calm down for what felt like five minutes, so I started to unwind with a jigsaw puzzle in the dining room. The day was going so smoothly until Emma found me.

Once again, I was faced with her demanding answers, insisting she go to the police about the domestic abuse. I was running out of ways to put her off, so I tried explaining how scared I was that Richard would do something horrific. It didn't seem to work because all she did then was push and push until it drove me absolutely crazy.

The only thing I could think of was to stall – to make up some story about why Richard didn't like having people in his office. It was completely fictitious, of course. The real reason he didn't want anyone in there was because it was the one place he could hide from me and block out the world. See, he had a key, and I didn't.

You can guess how much that angered me.

While this story rolled off the tongue, I started to think of what else I could tell her. It was a matter of mere seconds or minutes before she would press even harder for an explanation, picking Katie as her focus. Well, I wasn't about to tell her the truth, and I had completely run out of ideas, so I delayed things by telling her there was something to see upstairs.

It gave me a few minutes to conjure something, but it still wasn't coming.

'These belonged to Katie,' I said, letting her into the room. 'Come and see.'

While Emma perused Katie's belongings – which, I might add, we had hidden during the police search on our property and were too scared to throw away in case they were found – I tried to think outside the box. Maybe, I thought, feeding her story after story was no longer the best course of action. What if getting rid of her was the solution? It would be a weird kind of irony that she would share a similar fate to Katie, and all because of her own *interest* in Katie. Sure, it was risky, but it was certainly easier.

'You said this was the first thing that made you think she died,' Emma said, glancing up from the suitcase of things long enough to look at me. 'What's the second?'

'Ah. Yes.'

I went to the bedroom window then, my heart throbbing as I desperately thought of a way out. It was only then, staring out at our very own garden, that I finally understood the answer. It was so obvious, and as long as I executed things to perfection, it was going to be easy.

Emma listened well as I told her about Richard. I made some things up and changed some others, but it wasn't important. What *was* important was how much she believed me. All I had to do was give her some hope. Make her think she could get her answers once and for all if only she would go out and visit the well.

She did, of course, and I went right out there after her. Honestly, I thought she was going to hear me coming through the crunchy, snow-coated grass or see my shadow stretch across the well like a lunging monster. I guess that's what I was, after all, because I didn't hesitate to catch up to her and shove her in the back. I just waited for her to lean over a little – just enough to sacrifice some balance – and then I did the deed.

Emma didn't scream as she went down. Not a single sound left her mouth. There was just a quick scrape of her skin against the brick, and then she plummeted to the bottom like I'd said Katie did. The next thing I heard was a thud as she hit the bottom.

Finally, my problem was solved: Emma was officially out of the picture.

And she wasn't coming back.

Chapter Twenty

NORA

The feeling that comes after is nothing short of exhilarating. It's like an adrenaline rush, all my senses dialling up to eleven – like I've just taken a hit of cocaine and couldn't possibly sit down and rest even if I tried. So much nervous energy is building up inside me that I have to keep pacing the house as my mind races, figuring out what I'm going to tell everyone.

The first and most important thing is to make sure Jacob didn't see out of his window because that will ruin everything. I head right upstairs and catch him sitting on a beanbag in the corner of his room. The window is not too far from him, and if he sat up at any given moment, he could have witnessed the whole thing. Although I must admit, judging from how deeply his nose is buried in that book, he's probably completely oblivious.

'Enjoying yourself over there, young man?' I ask from the doorway. I'm trying to lean against the door frame casually, but my son and I talk so rarely that I don't really know how to communicate with him. It comes out all stiff and stilted.

'Yes, Mummy,' he says without looking up.

'What's it about?'

Although he answers, I don't hear a word. My attention is gobbled up by the window. I make my way towards it while he rambles on, seeing the well from a distance and feeling that rush of electric excitement all over again. *I just killed Emma*, I think.

I just killed *Emma!*

'Can I carry on?' Jacob asks.

'What?' I turn to look down at him, and he simply raises the book a couple of inches in the air. 'Oh. Yes. Listen, Emma won't be coming back today. She might not be here tomorrow or the next day either, so read as much as you like and be a good little boy, okay?'

Jacob's face creases up with confusion, but who

has time to address it? Richard will soon be asking what happened to our son's tutor, and if I don't get in there quickly, then I'll have little to no control over what he believes.

We can't have that now, can we?

I find him down in the office. He opens the door and looks at me as though I'm something he stood in, but I'm too busy putting on my best performance to react to it. The heavy breathing shows as my chest heaves up and down, and I talk in short, panting sentences.

'You need to run,' I say, pointing up the hall. 'She left. Emma. She...'

'Calm down.' Richard leans out of the room and follows the direction of my pointed finger, burying his hate for me just so he can get to the bottom of this mystery. 'What do you mean, she left? Has she gone back into town?'

'I think so. It's still icy. It's not safe.'

'She'll be all right.'

'No, she'll slip and fall.'

'I doubt she's dumb enough to try the impossible twice.'

'But she was looking all woozy as she went. I'm worried about her.'

Alarm registers in his face. 'Do you know which direction she went?'

'Down the main road, maybe.'

Richard looks over his shoulder, hesitating for only a second before taking command. He whips his jacket off the back of his seat, locks the door, then storms down the hall while going straight for the cloakroom. 'Stay with Jacob,' he says, every bit the guardian of this dysfunctional little family. 'If she comes back, turn on the upstairs lights so I can see from down the hill. Whatever you do, don't follow me.'

Seconds later, he leaves the house in search of our hired help. I stand in the hall and smile, watching through the porch window as he carefully heads through the main gate and embarks on his journey down the hill in search of Emma.

He'll never find her.

Long before Richard returns, Jacob ventures out of his bedroom and down the stairs. The book he's been carrying around for a while is nowhere to be seen. Instead of that giddy insistence on returning to his little world of fiction, he's all frowns.

'What's the matter with you?' I ask, then return my focus to the window. There's still no sign of my husband, and I wonder how long he's going to spend down there before returning empty-handed. And believe me, he *will* be empty-handed.

'Do you think Emma will ever come back?' Jacob asks.

'I don't know.'

'But did she say where she was going?'

'No.'

'She was my favourite. Do you think she liked me, too?'

'I don't know, Jacob.'

'But do you think—'

'Jacob, *I do not know!*'

My son shrinks back as I whirl away from the window. His arms come up as if to defend himself from a malicious strike, and my heart races at the idea of hurting him. Where did this new sensation come from? Why am I suddenly finding it so hard to control my impulses?

It all started with Katie, I suppose.

'Mummy didn't mean to raise her voice,' I say, dropping to my knees and easing my tone to show him I'm not a threat. 'Why don't you come and have a cuddle? Everything is always much better after a cuddle, don't you think?'

Jacob is hesitant, caution flaring in his eyes. When he does finally move towards me, he does so slowly and lets me embrace him, but he doesn't hug me back. Instead, he just cries onto my shoulder with that pathetic little snivel.

'I really, *really* miss Emma,' he says.

'I know.'

'Please make her come back.'

That's not likely, I think with a bizarre amount of pride. To tell the truth, it's really starting to piss me off that he's so infatuated with his tutor. Emma was hired to do a job, nothing more, and Jacob is supposed to love *me*. Not Emma, certainly not Katie or Richard, but *me*. I have no idea what it's going to take to win back his affections, but if it takes that much work, I'd rather not go through the hassle. After all, I'm his mother. If he doesn't love me naturally, then he shouldn't love me at all, and if that latter part is the case, then... well...

There are more problems in our immediate future.

. . .

Richard makes it home just before dark, freezing cold and exasperated. He knows better than to ask for my aid, so he helps himself to a cup of coffee and stands above the scalding radiator to warm his hands. I keep my distance from him, standing at the boiling saucepan and giving it the occasional stir. I do my best to look concerned for our tutor's well-being.

'You didn't find her?' I ask, sounding hopeless.

'No, and nobody in town has seen her either.'

'Do you think she got lost along the way?'

'Not if she just went back down the hill.'

'She might have slipped on the ice.'

'Then I'd have found her. It's not exactly easy to lose your way, is it?' Richard rubs his hands together, then turns to let some heat drift up the back of his shirt. 'It's one long, straight road with nothing but short grass on either side. Are you absolutely sure she went that way?'

I do my best to look puzzled, recounting what I said to him earlier today. Did I tell him I saw Emma, or did I just say she intended to go down the path? I have to choose my next words carefully. 'There's no reason to think otherwise.'

Richard nods and says no more until we're seated at the dinner table as a family.

'I've been thinking about what you said,' he tells me, setting his fork down gently with half the food still left on his plate. 'About Emma looking... what was the word you used?'

'Woozy,' I remind him.

'Right. But her wound was healed by then. So what was wrong with her?'

I reached for a glass of wine and took a long sip, half to savour the fruity richness, half to give me enough time to think. It's obvious he's suspicious about my story – he wouldn't be asking questions otherwise – and my lies are getting thinner every time I open my mouth.

'She didn't say,' I manage in the end, shredding a bit of tender meat and swilling it in the hot gravy. It's mostly just to keep my hands busy. My appetite is suddenly out the window. 'Maybe there's nothing to worry about. She'll come back, I think.'

'Really?' Jacob pipes up, springing to life.

'Maybe.'

'Good. Emma is my best friend.'

I shoot him a look and tell him to eat his dinner, but he doesn't seem to be hungry either. He's been playing with his food for a while, and I don't mind this interaction with him because it's a good distraction from Richard and his questions.

Except Richard doesn't want to leave it alone.

'Okay, buddy,' he says to Jacob. 'If you're not hungry, you can go read.'

'No,' I say, the worry starting to spread. 'He has to eat.'

'Not if he isn't hungry.'

'A young man like that should—'

'Nora.' Richard stares daggers at me, and I think he knows – *oh God, he knows!* – but he's sending Jacob to his room because it will leave the two of us alone. It works, too, because Jacob leaves with a big smile, and Richard studies me like a book. Suddenly, my threats to him seem useless. 'There's something you're not telling me.'

I shake my head. 'No. What makes you say that?'

'We both know Emma didn't have time to get down that hill.'

'Then maybe she went a different way.'

'Like what? Through the woods?'

'Potentially.'

'There's a problem with that theory.' Richard shoves his plate to one side and leans forward, resting his strong chin on interlaced fingers. 'Since you've been filling her head up with lies, the only reason she could possibly have to risk hurting herself again is to tell the police. But see, I know you wouldn't want that to happen because then you'd be at risk as well. You know that, don't you? You're cruel and frightening, maybe even deluded, but not stupid.'

I shake my head once more. 'You're being silly.'

'Don't gaslight me!'

Richard slams a fist on the table so hard that the cutlery leaves the plate, and a few drops of wine splash out of my glass. I reach for it and use it to hide my fear – my panic that he's going to find out the truth and have me arrested. That would be perfect for him, wouldn't it? Then he could live happily ever after with our son while I take the blame for what happened to Katie. That's not something I want to happen.

I can't let him win.

'Well?' he says through gritted teeth.

'Well what?'

'Are you going to tell me the truth?'

I thought about it. Of course I did. But this whole situation is getting messier and messier. The more Richard knows, the more he has against me, so for now, it's best he just thinks Emma has gone. Jacob can take yet another break from schooling, and we can relax for a while without people badgering us about Katie's whereabouts.

'That's the truth,' I say. 'Take it or leave it, but it won't change.'

Richard eyes me sceptically, his eyes digging right through me. I can't stand to look at him, so I pierce some meat and green beans onto my fork and then shovel it into my mouth, only looking up at him from time to time and trying to play it cool.

Eventually, he sighs, scoots back the chair, then leaves the room. It's hard to say whether I've got away with it or not, but I recently found something that will keep me safe if he ends up going anywhere near that well. In spite of everything, I don't want him to leave me. And if we can't be together in life, then I'll just have to visit his office and take that rifle off the wall.

Then, we can all be together as a happy family forever.

Not in life but in death.

Chapter Twenty-One

I am alive.

Barely.

The fall down the well wasn't as simple as it sounds. The jagged, bumpy outcroppings of brick tore at my hands as I reached for something to cling to. My feet scuffed against them halfway through, my ankle twisting and slowing my fall. When I hit the dark, terrifying bottom, the weak ice acted as a barrier to keep me from striking the stone beneath it. That's not to say it didn't hurt like hell, but the simple fact remains.

I am alive.

For now.

Although I'm also broken. I don't think I've moved since those first five minutes, where I slowly and agonisingly sat up. The shattered ice beneath me wasn't that deep, so I managed to hoist myself onto a lump of rock and just sat there.

I'm still here now, hugging my knees to my chest and hoping to get warm. The sun went away a little while ago, and the cold is really starting to set in. Except for my backside, everything from the knee up is still dry, and the wind can't get to me down here. Even if the snow started up again, I wouldn't know it because the well has a small roof. The downside to that, of course, is that the sun also won't reach me down here. It's horrifically cold at the bottom of an ice-filled stone well when you have wet feet.

But intense though it may be, the pain isn't my only problem. There's also the fear factor, sitting down here while something may be broken or sprained, wondering if I'm ever going to be found. The walls feel like they're closing in on me, and they were never that far apart to begin with. All I can do all night is shiver uncontrollably and think. I think about Richard and his abusive ways, about Katie and the fact her body isn't down here, and about Nora.

Nora, who lied.

But why would she do such a thing? If Katie

isn't at the bottom of this well – and I know for a fact she isn't because I can perform a thorough search in all of four seconds – then where is she now? Is what Nora said about her husband even true? Is any of it? Another question keeps circling my mind, like a scavenging crow ready to feed on my shock.

Is Katie really dead?

While I shudder, starve, and cry, that's all I can seem to focus on. Not only did one tutor go missing, but now somebody in that house wants me out of the picture, too. I think back to when I was pushed, going over and over the one small detail that stood out to me ever since getting pushed. Richard is a big guy, his hands huge and strong. A man's hands.

But those aren't what shoved me.

I felt the small, delicate little palms strike my back. I heard the grunt as my attacker threw all their strength into knocking me off balance. They weren't the hands of a man at all – they were the hands of a frightened little housewife who, for whatever reason, wanted me gone.

Which brings me to my next question.

Why?

. . .

I'm alone with these thoughts in the black of night. The only glint of light I see is a thin beam of the moon's glow bouncing off a high brick and reflecting into the icy water by my feet. My body is stiff and aching, the pain in my ankle getting too much. It's hard to say if it's broken or if I just haven't moved in a long time. Regardless, it's excruciating.

I've been listening to the wind, too. How it echoes as it sweeps up the great hill. It's terrifying. I feel like a survivor stuck under some rubble, waiting for the final collapse that will end it all. Although in my case, the collapse would come in the form of either starvation or the extreme cold. Maybe I should count my blessings. If this had happened two days ago, the frost would have already finished me off.

By now, I would be dead.

But the fact is I'm not, which brings about more questions: what if Nora wants to come and finish me off? Does she even know I'm still alive? If not, how long will it stay that way? Why did she do this to me in the first place? How much of what she said was true?

My head hurts from the overthinking. I try distracting myself with the sounds of the world outside. The brushing of the wind, the swaying of the trees. It's like music, the bassline not a thumping but more of a gentle crunching. I listen closer, trying to discern what that noise is, and it takes all of thirty seconds to figure it out.

It's feet crunching on frosty grass.

Somebody is up there.

'Hello?' I say, my voice a stuttering echo. 'Nora, is that you?'

The silence is killing me faster than the cold ever could. I wait in dreaded anticipation of her voice, calling down to tell me the truth about why I was cast down here to suffer... or to die. But when a voice does finally call back, it's not hers at all.

It's Richard's.

'Emma?' he says. 'Emma, are you down there?'

'Yeah, it's me.'

To tell the truth, I don't know what to think. Everything I've seen or heard about this man is enough to make any woman run a mile. Any woman except Nora, that is. But exactly how much of it is true? If she had the nerve to shove me into a well and try to kill me, something tells me she's hardly playing with a full deck.

'Jesus Christ,' he mutters. 'What the hell happened? Are you hurt?'

'I don't know. I think so. My ankle hurts.'

'How long have you been down there?'

'No idea. Since earlier today, maybe.'

Richard goes quiet then. *Too* quiet. My neck clicks as I strain to look up, fighting to see the opening of the well. There is a figure there, the moon faintly announcing his outline. He hasn't run away yet. Good.

'Did Nora do this to you?' he asks, sounding desperate and sincerely shocked.

'If it wasn't you, then yes, she did it.'

'I'm not the guy you think I am, Emma.'

'No? Then prove it by getting me out of here.'

'I will, I will. It's just...'

That pause makes me uncomfortable. He doesn't need to tell me I'm not about to be rescued because the doubt is evident in his voice. No, not doubt – fear. It's the same thing I heard from Nora so many times. A breathless, hurried sort of panic. One of these two is very good at acting, and considering I'm stuck down here, I'll bet it's Nora.

'Richard,' I say, trying to sound calm yet forceful. 'Get me out of here right now.'

'It's not that simple,' he says. 'If Nora...'

'If Nora *what*, for crying out loud?'

'Don't you see? She's completely lost her mind.

All those bumps and bruises you found on her – the cut, too – were all self-inflicted to make me look like the bad guy because she... well, Katie... Look, I couldn't say anything because she keeps threatening to take Jacob away from me or hurt him. If I get you out of here and she sees you...'

My heart is racing, my brain looking back over the past few days like a superfast rewind. I picture the bruise on her wrist, the cut, the bloody nose she later covered in makeup. But I also recall the blunt abruptness with which Richard always spoke. Looking back now, was he just trying to distance himself from me and Nora? Was he trying not to get too involved so there would be less of a mess to clean up when she was done telling lies?

Richard tells me everything. About the smoking, the gossiping, and how hard he tried to make her stop hurting herself. He tells me about the threats she made (and still makes) because she's desperate to cover up what happened with my predecessor. I want to ask about that and finally get the truth, but right now, my focus is on getting out of here.

'So you're not a bad guy after all,' I say, sucking up to him a little.

'Not at all. But that doesn't mean I can save you.'

'*What?*'

'Like I said, she can't see you.'

I sit up straight, no longer caring when my foot plunges into the ice water. I tilt my head back again to gape up at him, suddenly panicking that the cavalry hasn't come after all. 'Richard, you can't leave me down here to die. I can go into town. I can get help or even just leave town and never return. Nora doesn't have to know about it.'

'But you said your ankle hurts.'

'It does, but—'

'Then you'll never make it back.'

'All right, then get me out of here and do your Nightingale routine.'

'I can't.'

'Richard, you're a doctor, for crying out loud. Help me!'

The well goes quiet again, just like it has been for hours. I stir in the water, the sloshing sound rising up the walls and through the top like a funnel. I'm waiting for him to act – to change his mind and let the pail down to help me out of here.

It never happens.

'I'm sorry,' he says solemnly. 'I just can't. But I'll be back. Trust me.'

'Richard, no.' Silence. 'Richard? *Richard!*'

That's the last time I hear his voice, and I'm left to angrily slam my fist into the stone. It doesn't bother me that my skin splits and draws blood. I was just offered a way out, and then it was taken from me just as quickly as it'd come along. My breath is coming out in short, panicked little gusts that feel like my lungs are being squeezed. I should know this feeling, as it's not the first time I've felt it since falling down the well.

It's the feeling of knowing I'm going to die.

When he says he'll be back, I don't know if that means in an hour or a day.

Or at all.

There's no way to tell how much time is passing as every little shiver rips through my body like slow, deliberate torture. Every little howl of wind stretches on for an eternity. Every thought I've had spirals round and round until it's driving me insane.

Not surprisingly, the tears come again. I never was one to feel sorry for myself, but a person can't help it when facing death. It's in our nature to lose something – in this case, life – and look back at all the things that could have been. All the things we *would* have achieved and, most of all, the people who would miss us.

I don't have anyone like that. All of my relationships came to fail. All of my friends got married and had kids, putting their focus into those rather than hanging out with poor little Emma. Even my family no longer keeps in touch, and honestly, it makes me feel a little pathetic. That might be why I travel – I like to stay on the road, bury myself in work, and move on before people get a chance to tell me they can't stay friends with me.

It's a sad little existence, really.

Not that it'll be much of a problem any more.

The tears start to come harder. Under the circumstances, I think it's okay to allow a little self-pity. Ever since coming up to this hill, all I ever wanted to do was help people. Jacob with his education. Nora with her fictional domestic abuse. See where that got me?

Knocking on death's door, that's where. And unless Richard hurries back to get me out of here, that's where I'm going to stay. I'm so desperate for escape that I'm starting to imagine his voice.

Jacob's, too. They're calling out to me over and over, but they'll never come.

'Emma? Emma!'

It's all in my head.

I'm going to die.

Chapter Twenty-Two

By morning, my hate for Nora has greatly intensified. I can't stop going over and over all of this in my head, picturing her bruises and cuts and the award-worthy performance she's been giving this whole time. I feel like an idiot. Not just because I fell for it all but because I actually went out of my way to help that psychopath. It's hard to believe she can hurt herself that badly. And for what? To get at Richard? Sure, but why?

A few hours ago, I had the good sense to remove my socks and shoes. It's funny: it doesn't feel like the right thing to do, exposing my feet to the blistering cold, but the icy water in the weave of my socks was starting to make my toes numb. I can't stop thinking about frostbite and all those stories I've heard over the years. I'd worry about losing my feet to it, but there are bigger things to concern myself with right now.

Like getting out of here at all.

Just as the sun rises, so does Richard's outline at the top of the well. I really don't know if I'm hallucinating now – this is the most tired I've ever been in my life, and hunger is starting to twist knots in the depths of my stomach.

'Emma?' he says, his voice echoing like the Voice of God. 'Are you...?'

'I'm alive,' I tell him moodily. 'No thanks to you.'

'Yes, well, I want to help.'

'Then you can start by getting me out of here.'

Richard sighs. I squint, adjusting my eyes to the brightness of the sun as it peeks over the horizon behind him. He's thinking, and I don't want to interrupt that. Not if it's going to give me a fighting chance of making it through the day.

'Listen,' he says at long last. 'I can get you out, but you can't go back to Wedchester.'

'That's fine. The quicker I leave, the better.'

'No, I mean you can't leave the property.'

'What?' I stand up again, putting my foot right back in the water and wincing with pain as the cold bites my skin like a piranha. 'Why the hell not?'

'I told you, we can't risk Nora hurting Jacob. If she sees you running into town, or if you contact the police, she's going to take him away from me. Even if she doesn't manage to pin her crimes on me, I'm scared to death that she'll do something nasty. Something stupid.'

It's odd to hear that this big, burly man is so afraid of a tiny little woman like Nora. But I know how this works by now; she's told her lies, tainted his image, and now he's caught between a rock and a hard place. Much like I am, except for him it's a figure of speech.

'What crimes?' I ask.

'What?'

'You said she'll pin her crimes on you. What did she do?'

Silence greets me once more, leaving me to ponder. Obviously, Katie crosses my mind.

'Okay,' he says. 'If I get you out of here, you need to promise you'll stay in the barn.'

'How long for?'

'Until I can figure out what to do.'

'Can't you just... kill her?'

'Despite what she's told you, I'm not a monster.'

Now it's my turn to sigh. It comes out in a long, shivery breath that hurts my lungs. They still feel tight, just like all my joints. I'd do anything to get out of here, but what I really want to do is run into town and scream to the nearest person who will listen.

'Can I have a change of clothes?' I ask.

'I have some right here. Blankets, too.'

'And food?'

'In the same bag. You need to promise, Emma. I'm not risking Jacob's life.'

I give it some thought. Can I really sit in a barn like a good little girl while Richard figures out how to save his son? The selfish part of me wants to make the promise and then run as fast as I can, but this is Jacob we're talking about. Sweet, innocent little Jacob. He never did anything wrong to anyone, so why should he suffer in all of this?

'Fine,' I tell Richard. My decision is made. 'I promise.'

Getting me out of the well is anything but easy. It's nothing like you'd imagine: one leg is wobbly as

I plant my foot into the lowered pail. Splinters pierce my skin, but they're of little importance right now.

My concentration is better spent maintaining my balance as Richard heaves me up with all his strength. Meanwhile, I'm using my free leg to press against the well wall, keeping myself from spinning out of control. I don't like heights, so fear burns through every ounce of my body as the rope moans at my weight. I'm getting higher now, closer to the top. Closer to freedom, or as close to freedom as I can get without going back to town.

The sun burns my eyes as I emerge from my prison. It's cresting over the top of the house, the harsh orange stinging so bad I have to turn my head. Richard makes sure I have a good grip on the side of the well, then releases the rope and heaves me out of there.

'Won't Nora see this?' I ask.

'She's in the bath, but we have to be quick.'

'Can't I try making a run for it?'

'Emma—'

'Yeah... I know.'

Richard bends over to pick something up. My eyes are quickly adjusting to the light, but I shield them with my hand all the same. Next thing I know, a warm blanket is draped over my shoulders. I lower my hand and hug it close while Richard rubs my arms.

'Come on, let's get you inside.'

'I won't fight you.'

Making use of our limited time, Richard reaches for a carrier bag full of things and then puts an arm around me, helping me move across the snow-crusted grass. It hurts to walk, and the cold doesn't help. Having no shoes on is another complication – I left those at the bottom of the well. Good riddance. I just hope there are spares in the bag.

When we get back to the barn, he closes the door behind us and directs me to a bed of hay. It stinks in here, like animals that I can't tell if they're dead or alive. Regardless, there are none here. I'm just glad to have somewhere warm to stay.

Richard rummages through the bag, fishing out a whole bunch of clothes – and shoes, thank God – along with two big bottles of water and a whole bunch of fruit and packaged savoury goods. It's not much, but it means the world to someone as hungry as me.

'The snow will thaw soon,' he tells me. 'It's mostly gone, but I went down there looking for you and fell on my arse three times. When it melts a little more, we can start thinking about you going back to town and doing... whatever it is you should do.'

'Like call the police?'

'Well, maybe we shouldn't.'

'It's not my business, Richard, but your son can't live in constant danger.'

'There you go. Something we can agree on.'

'So what else is there to think about?'

'How to get there without Nora seeing you.'

I take the food onto the hay, throwing myself down and tearing open a banana peel. It's in my mouth and down my throat in less than ten seconds, forcing me to talk with a full mouth. 'I could go at night. When she's sleeping.'

Richard shakes his head. 'That's when the ice is at its worst.'

'Why don't you distract her?'

'It's not just that. What about when the police come up the hill?'

'Right. She'll see them from a mile off.'

Richard sighs and rakes a hand through his hair while I reach for an apple, biting into the crispy peel as juice runs down my chin. I'm seeing him in a whole new light now, and I'm not just talking about the sunrays beaming up his face in slats.

Once you strip away the pre-installed idea that he's a violent, controlling abuser, it's easy to see a man who cares very deeply for the well-being of his son. A young boy I've even come to adore myself.

I just hope I can keep him out of trouble and, with Richard's help, figure out a way to get out of this situation without anyone getting hurt. Although, from what the searing pain in my ankle reports, Nora is a force to be reckoned with. It means we shouldn't just be careful.

We should be afraid.

Look, I know it's wrong, but I can't help myself.

After spending such a long time freezing my arse off, the immobility leaves me feeling depressed. It's not like I can go running up and down a steep, icy road in the middle of the night, but at least I can wander the length of the barn and try to get some sense of feeling back into my toes. Frankly, it's a miracle I can stand. Much less walk.

The problem is I want to do that one thing.

The thing I shouldn't, under any circumstances.

Night falls by the time I get some feeling back in my toes. The spare clothes help a ton, and after taking a thorough assessment from Richard, I'm assured there's no risk of frostbite. Apparently, it was cold enough to hurt, and my ankle had simply taken a hard knock.

Nothing is broken.

I can't stop thinking about Jacob. We didn't have much time to bond, but I grew very fond of him in the short space of time we were together. He's such an endearing boy, which only makes it worse that his parents don't pay him much attention. It's a bit more understandable with Richard – anything he says or does is just used against him by his psycho wife. As for Nora, well... it's obvious her son's needs are second to her own. That's generally what happens when you're a vindictive narcissist.

For as long as I'm thinking about him, I want to make sure he's all right. How am I supposed to know that something hasn't happened inside that house? I can't for sure, and that's why I make the stupid decision to step outside of the barn.

It's cold outside, but not as bad as it has been. The air is frosty and thin, but I bite back the pain and hurry over to the house. There are no lights on – no sign of anybody still awake, so it must be pretty late. I stop by all the windows, cupping my hands against the glass to peer in. Nothing has changed since my departure (death), which is a good sign.

After checking the windows one by one, I complete my walk around the house and start walking back towards the barn on sore heels. The front gate catches my eye, and I'm haunted by a memory of when I first caught a taxi up here, stupidly thinking my life was somehow about to get better rather than dangerously close to its end.

How dumb was I?

Now, facing the gate, I pay one last consideration to running down the hill and crying for help. I doubt Nora would know about it until the police come to investigate, but what if I didn't report it? I could go right now – it would be so easy – and just grab my stuff from the bed and breakfast, then leave town without looking back. Not my family, not my problem.

Only it *is* my problem. I made a promise to help kids, and that doesn't stop with their education. Even if not as a tutor, then as a good human being, I have a moral obligation to help a child in need. I mean, if I can't help him, then who will? Sure, it would be easier to just flee the scene and start a new life somewhere far away, but how could

I live with myself knowing I'd left a young boy with some nutcase on an isolated hilltop?

No, Jacob deserves better, and he's going to get just that.

Until then, I must stay in the barn and be patient.

Chapter Twenty-Three

It comes as a surprise that I get a good night's sleep. The hay is warm but scratchy, and the concrete floor beneath it is hard and cold. Still, between all these layers and a dusty old pillow I found in a box at the back of the barn, I manage to drift into a dream world, the awful conditions of that well now just a bitter, distant memory.

I dream of home, as I usually do when facing dark times. Perhaps it's my happy place – my happy childhood acting like a refuge when times are hard. My family were the best of them, my mother a teacher like me and my father running his own carpentry business. My sister was always confused, never quite feeling happy in her line of work, but her heart was good and her intentions pure. She and I argued a lot, but we always made it up to each other by later coming back to admit when we realised we were wrong. My parents and I didn't argue at all until the very end. That's why it came as such a shock when they separated – Mum and Dad split, and suddenly, they were no longer interested in their grown-up daughters.

It looks like that's not such a happy place after all.

When I wake up, the barn is warm and quiet. I shove a layer off me, test the temperature of the room, then get to my feet and start stretching. Most of my pain is gone, but the ripped skin on my leg still stings when my trouser fabric catches it wrong. I don't mind much.

At least I'm safe.

Almost as if to read my mind and prove me wrong, the peace is broken by commotion somewhere outside the barn. I run to the door, only slightly limping and slamming to a stop when I press my face against the wood. There's a hole here, just big enough to see through. I peek and look around for the source of the noise, quickly finding it at the house.

Richard is there, standing on the back patio where Nora used to smoke. Right in front of him,

Nora is jerking her finger at his chest and screaming something. I can't make out what she's saying, but it's clear she's got a bee in her bonnet about something.

My breath is caught in my throat. I'm wondering if she's found out that I'm still alive, being helped by her husband as he plots against her. At first, I think that's silly and over the top, but she soon comes storming towards the door, her angry voice growing louder.

I want to watch and listen, but I can't.

She'll catch me if I don't hide.

The first thing I do is rush to grab the bag and clothes from the hay. Panicking, I scrunch it all together and hold it close to my chest. Then, I run to the back of the barn and hide inside a bay, keeping as still and quiet as possible in the dark.

The voices grow louder as they close the distance.

'I'm not hiding anything from you!' Richard yells. 'You're so paranoid!'

'Then why do you keep going into the garden?'

'I'm making a gift for you! It's supposed to be a surprise!'

Silence.

Then Nora breaks it. 'A surprise? What kind of a surprise?'

'It wouldn't be much of a surprise if I told you.'

'Well, is it in here?'

I wait, terrified, as Richard makes up his mind. Whatever he says next will either drive her away from the barn or right into it. My mind wanders to what she'll do if she catches me – how she will hurt Jacob, and the only way to stop her would be to hurt her. A small, rogue part of me wants to do it, but Richard would never let it happen.

No wonder she managed to manipulate him so easily.

'No, actually,' he finally says. 'It's in the woods. Not far from the well.'

'What?' Nora sounds suspicious. 'You went near the well?'

'Yes, why?'

'No reason.'

'No? Maybe I should go and take a look, then.'

Nora panics, both their voices fading into the distance while he bluffs to get her away from the barn. *Very clever*, I think with a smile, finally letting out the breath that was about to burst my lungs. It's scary how close I just came to being caught, and even though I'm glad to get away with it, it does beg the question.

How long can we do this?

A WHOLE DAY PASSES, and Richard hasn't brought me any more food.

I'm starting to stretch it out, eating some Pringles here, a pear there. Without knowing how long I'm going to be stuck in hiding, it's imperative I make it last. It would be a shame to come this far and then die of starvation like some wild animal.

I'm keeping an eye on the snow, too, using that hole in the wood to monitor its progress. It's almost completely thawed, which means the road should be clear of ice. If not, then it won't be long now. Not that it means I can leave, but if it comes to it...

That said, it's about time I start making a plan. I can't spend my life shut up in a barn while the world goes on without me. Jacob still needs protecting, Richard deserves vindication, and Katie... well, there are people out there who'll want to know what happened.

Though I'm starting to get a good idea. After everything I've heard from different people in that family, it's not a stretch to suggest that the private tutor is long gone. Dead, probably. The real question is who killed her. Nora? Most likely.

The day goes on like that. There's nothing to do, so I just theorise over and over while the sun slowly melts away the snow. I snack occasionally, staring hard at the door while my body goes through the recovery process. I'm exhausted, dying for a good night's sleep in a bed. Not just any old bed either – a warm bed in a safe environment.

As if from nowhere, a click sounds across the barn. I freeze, my heart skipping a beat while my mind races through a thousand possibilities of what caused it. But when I see the barn door open and the sunlight bleed in, it all becomes clear.

Nora has figured it out.

THE MOVEMENT COMES SO FAST it scares the hell out of me. As soon as the door is open, the shadowy shape comes sprinting through the sudden burst of sunlight, arms akimbo. My leg moves of its own accord as if to start running, but there's nowhere to go. Even if there was, there's no reason to. Because my eyes adjust, and I can make out who it is.

'Emma!' Jacob yells, slamming into me and almost knocking me over.

I drop to my knees and hold him tight, enjoying the small amount of warmth his tiny body brings. There's dandruff in his messy hair, which immediately makes me think he's not being taken care of. No wonder this kid likes me so much – I'm the only one who gives a damn about him. At least as far as he can tell.

'I thought you were dead,' he says as he squeezes me.

'Why would you think that?'

'Mummy said you weren't coming back.'

I pull away and put my hands on his shoulders to look him in the eye, then notice the barn door is wide open. I rush over to it, glance up at the house (not knowing if we're being watched), and then pull the door shut. The light blinks out in the bat of an eye, and I take a moment to let my heartbeat settle. It's so good to see Jacob again.

'What's going on back in the house?' I ask, taking his hand and leading him to a nearby stepladder where he can sit on the metal run. 'Your mum and dad must be acting pretty strangely up there. Have you noticed anything different about them?'

Jacob taps his lower lip as he thinks. 'Hmm...'

'Anything at all?'

'Mummy is angrier than usual.'

'How so?'

'Well, she's started throwing things. She always shouts at Daddy.'

'Okay. What does he do?'

Jacob shrugs.

'Come on,' I prompt. 'He must do *something*.'

'Yeah, that's what I'm showing you.' He shrugs again. 'Daddy does this.'

Now I get it. Richard tries not to react to his batshit crazy wife, shrugging it off. Leaving the room. Raising his voice when he has to, but never in front of their kid. Just like he never used to shout in front of me. It just goes to show how deceiving appearances can be.

'Jacob, has she shouted at you at all?'

'Mmm, nope.'

'Not even a little bit?'

'Nope. But she does tell me off for talking about you.'

'Really?' It's such an odd thing for Nora to do, but it doesn't surprise me like you'd think it would. After all, it's recently come to light that she's a liar and – very possibly – a killer. 'What exactly does she say when she tells you off?'

Jacob looks down at his hands, picking under

his fingernails. 'That you're not my mum. That I'm not allowed to get upset about you leaving because *she's* my mum and I have to love her. *Only* her. So she said she'll take away my books if I talk about you again.'

'Honey, you haven't done anything wrong. Your mum is going through some stuff.'

'What do you mean? Like when she went through Daddy's stuff?'

'No.' I shake my head, not at all surprised to learn she's done that. 'I mean, life is really hard for her at the moment. Sometimes when that happens, people start to act a little different. It's not a reflection on you, okay? It just means she's having a hard time.'

'Should I pick her some flowers?'

'Probably best not to let her know you've been in the garden.'

'Why?'

'Because it will draw attention to me.'

'Why is that a bad thing?'

'Because...'

I cut myself off right there, suddenly remembering I'm talking to a six-year-old. There's no need for him to know that his mother tried to kill me. It's best he thinks I'm playing some sort of game, but how can I do that without telling him the truth? And how can I keep him out of harm's way? It does cross my mind that I could take him right now – make a run for it down the hill with him at my side or in my arms. Richard is a big boy, so he can take care of himself. The idea fizzes in my excited mind for an instant.

Then I remember.

Nora's eyes when she spotted the rifle on the wall.

Best not to take any chances.

'Listen.' I take Jacob's hands and kneel in front of him, letting him know how serious this is. 'I'm planning a huge surprise for your mum. I told her I was leaving so she would think I'm not here any more, so you mustn't tell her you found me.'

'What's the surprise?'

'If I tell you, it won't be a secret any more.'

'But I won't tell anyone.'

'I believe you, but I still can't tell you.' *Mostly because I can't think of anything.* 'So you know what you should do? Keep your distance from Mummy for as long as possible. The more time you spend around her, the harder it will be to keep the secret. So just stay in your room like a good boy, okay? Promise me.'

Jacob smiles like this is all some big game. Ahh, the innocence of youth.

'But when will you give her the surprise?' he asks.

'Promise me, Jacob. Please.'

'Only if you tell me.'

I blow out an exasperated breath and make up some crap about having some of her old school friends come to stay. We're organising a party in the barn, I tell him, filling him with hope for jelly and ice cream. The look on his beaming face breaks my heart – the party will never come, but the most important thing is that he's going to steer clear of Nora.

'I promise,' he says after a lot of convincing.

Thankfully, I think I believe him.

Chapter Twenty-Four

A WHOLE DAY GOES BY. As soon as I'm awake, I clamber off my hay bed, dust myself off, then rush to the barn door and peer through the hole. This is the most excited I've ever been – the sun is out in full force, the grass sparkling with morning dew. There's a smell of crisp winter air, but there's no snow to boost its freezing temperature. The grass is green now, the road down to Wedchester totally free of ice. Which can only mean one thing.

Today, I can leave.

This is it. The day I get to return to town. The day I can have a hot shower and an equally hot meal. Only good things can come from my trip back to town, but I still don't know how to handle it. Richard is terrified that Nora might hurt his son, and I don't want to be the woman putting Jacob's life at risk. Leaving him with his mother isn't an option either, as there's no telling what she might do with enough time.

She's completely lost it.

Sometime into the afternoon, Richard comes to see me. I startle when the door opens, letting out a relieved breath as soon as he shows his face. There's no bag in his hand this time, but he's trying hard to smile through his stressed exterior.

'Where's Nora?' I ask, hoping he wasn't seen coming out here.

'She's having a nap.'

'Yeah, it must be exhausting being cuckoo.'

Richard nods, stuffs his hands in the pockets of his long, beige coat, then starts lazily dragging a blade of hay around under his foot. I've seen people do this before – usually when they're nervous. 'I was thinking today might be a good day for you to leave.'

'Good. That's what I thought.'

'Nora can't see you go. Remember, she probably thinks you're dead.'

'Then I'm guessing you don't want me to contact the police?'

'Absolutely not.'

'And Jacob...?'

'I'll take care of everything.'

I don't know what exactly he means by this, but I do know he's not a violent man. If there's any chance of Richard keeping his son safe, he'll need to pull some sort of magic trick. Nora, like most psychos, is a ticking time bomb, and they need to get as far away from her as possible. As *quickly* as possible.

'Are you sure that's what you want?' I ask. 'The police can be very discreet if I ask them to be. They could make their way up the hill without lights, and if you let them in, they don't even need to kick down any doors.'

'For what? A woman making a threat? They won't do anything.'

'They will if she's a danger to a child.'

'Not fast enough. Anyway, what if she blows up right in front of the police?'

'Then she'll be arrested.'

'But not before hurting someone.'

Richard says 'someone', but he means Jacob. I can see it in his eyes – the love he has for his child, just as any man should have. From the little I know of him, I'd bet he'll do anything to keep that kid safe. So would I, which is why I'm tempted to go against his orders and run straight to the cops. It couldn't be that dangerous... could it?

'Please promise me,' he says. 'I don't want you to cause any commotion.'

'What will you do, then? If I just go home?'

Richard shrugs, goes to the barn door, and rubs a hand over his head. He's looking down, taking deep, stressed breaths as he considers his options. 'I don't know. Maybe Nora will stop all this nonsense if I just play along with her.'

'Isn't that what you've been doing already?'

'Yes, but I could start acting like I'm madly in love with her, just like the good old days. I can buy her flowers, cook her romantic meals, keep telling her how much she means to me. In time, she might come to actually believe me.'

'But could *you?*'

'That doesn't matter.'

'It does though.' I go over to him, gently laying a hand on his shoulder, and wonder when was the last time someone actually looked out for him. 'You can't trick yourself into loving someone. Neither can you guarantee both you and Jacob won't get killed in your sleep.'

'It's not that bad.'

'It is, and you know it. See, you're already in denial.'

'Maybe that's what it will take.'

I slide my hand off him and sigh. There's no talking him round, so I gesture towards the door and encourage him to use it. 'You'd better get going. If she wakes up from her nap, then she might see you leaving here. Then you might actually have to make a surprise for her.'

Richard lazily huffs a fake laugh. 'If she finds you, that'll be surprise enough.'

'You're right.'

'Wait until nightfall, okay? When it's dark, get yourself down that hill and live your life. Just promise me you won't contact the police. I mean it, Emma. It's dangerous.'

He's not going to let me win this, so I might as well give up now. Whether or not I plan to keep it, I make the promise and send Richard on his way. Now I just have to find a way to kill time while I wait for night to come. It shouldn't be too hard.

There's plenty of thinking to do.

The rest of the day drags by so slowly I'm about to lose my mind.

It gets dark pretty early at this time of year, but it can't come soon enough. There are only so many times you can pace a barn, no matter how big it is, and I'm already getting tired. Hungry, too. Distressed. Cold. Angry. The list goes on.

To tell the truth, I still don't know whether to keep the promise. I told Richard the police won't be coming, but that was mostly to shut him up. It's easy to sympathise with a man in his position, and his fear is completely understandable. However, turning a blind eye to Nora's insane behaviour is dangerous. People like Nora tend to snap at some point or another. Who knows if that's going to be ten minutes from now or ten years?

Going out of my mind with worry, I head to the back of the barn and do some lunges just to get my blood circulating again. It helps to warm up, too, as well as burn off some of my nervous energy. My joints are stiff, my muscles sore, and my skin getting rough from overexposure to the cold. At least my ankle is starting to feel a little better – all I get is a faint ache when standing on that foot. Overall, things could be worse.

For instance, Nora could know I'm alive.

I wonder just how this is going to work. Even if I make it back to town without being seen, surely somebody will mention to Nora that they bumped into me. At some point, she's going to hear that I left. What will she do then? Accuse them of lying? Confess? Come looking for me or punish Richard and Jacob?

The more I think about it, the harder it is to keep that promise.

So, as awful as it may seem, I might not.

I just hope I'm doing the right thing.

Even when the sun goes down, it doesn't feel safe.

There's an overwhelming feeling like I'm being watched or as though this is all some sick game. I can almost imagine making my way to the open front gates as they call to me like a beacon, only to slam shut when I'm just inches away. A maniacal laugh would cackle behind me, and then Nora would come running at me with a knife. That might seem over the top to most people, but with my current string of bad luck, it's not impossible.

At least I can see what's going on in the house, to some degree. The brickwork itself bleeds with the blackness of the night sky behind it, but the rooms that still have lights on tell me a few things:

Jacob is in his room but not asleep; the kitchen is still in use; and the dining room light is on, although the curtains are drawn. I wonder if Nora is in there with her puzzle, drinking her grape juice just like she was when I last found her. Before she pushed me.

Before she killed me.

As far as she knows, that is.

It's tempting to leave right now, while I know where everyone is, but what's the harm in waiting a little longer? It's not like a few more minutes would make much of a difference to me, but Nora could show herself in one of the windows and give me a clear idea of where she is. I'd feel much more comfortable with cutting across the grass if that were the case.

The seconds turn to minutes, the minutes to an hour. My watch broke during the fall into the well, so I don't know what time it is, but it must be getting late. None of the lights have changed though, and my patience is wearing thin. When I see a slight shift of movement through the dining room curtain, I decide that maybe it's time to risk my escape. There's no time like the present, as they say.

It's now or never, say some others.

There's nothing to pack or carry – all of my things are either inside that house or in the bed and breakfast at the bottom of the hill – but I do put on as many layers as possible. Just because it's warmer than it was a few days ago doesn't mean it's warm. The wind is still howling outside, some leftover moisture still glazing the grass outside. By the time I'm ready to leave, I'm wearing two T-shirts, two cardigans, a coat, and a beanie that's so big it keeps slipping down my head to cover my eyes. It must be Richard's, I decide, ripping it off in case it blinds me at a critical moment. After all, I need all the help I can get.

Finally summoning up the courage to make my move, I exit the barn slowly. The wind fights against the door, and I close it carefully as it tries to swing shut. With the bitter wind sweeping across the garden and icily assailing my cheeks, I rush up to the house so as not to be seen from inside. Once there, I stick close to the wall and make my way around the building, my heart racing at every little sound I hear. There are too many noises – the whistling wind, the creaking trees as they sway under pressure, and the distant howl of some wolflike creature.

Great, I think while moving. *I'm stuck in a horror novel.*

Soon, I see the gate. Inching away from the house, I take a look back up at the windows and see some more lights have come on. I freeze as if they're headlights and I'm a deer, frightened stiff and unable to move. Even if it means saving my life. There's movement in the house, and now I don't know where it is, much less *who* it is.

There's no choice but to move. The gates are nearby. I sprint towards them, holding my breath the whole time. My lungs feel full to burst. I can see the twinkling lights of a pub down in Wedchester, which is the first place I'll go. Just to be around people, really – people who aren't trying to kill me. That will make for a pleasant change.

I'm so close to the gates that I can almost touch them. One of them is ajar, so it's definitely unlocked. It's inviting me – summoning me – to run through it and claim my liberation. I've never been so happy to be running, and I'm not going to stop until I have to. I want to get as far away from Nora as possible and—

The blast of a gunshot booms through the hill. Birds flee their nests. Richard screams from inside. I come to an immediate stop, a cold chill creeping under my layers and making my spine tingle with fear. I spin around, staring up at the house and knowing things just went from bad to worse. Nora found a gun – she must have – which means there's no time to run into town. But running inside would be suicide, especially if she has a weapon.

I suddenly remember the rifle on Richard's wall.

How Nora was eyeing it when she came into the office.

And how far she'll go to get what she wants.

Chapter Twenty-Five

NORA

THINGS HAVE BEEN WEIRD LATELY. I'm not talking about the kind of weird that makes you think there's something wrong with your spouse or that maybe they're planning some sort of early birthday surprise. What I mean is that Richard is up to something behind my back.

I hate it.

This all started when he began snooping around the barn. At first, I thought he was just looking for Emma (in which case, he just had to go a couple of hundred feet to his right and peer down the well), but then he started making repeat visits. One time, I saw him heading down the hall with a bag in his hand, but I didn't think to question it until it was too late. All I know is that he went into the garden with it, then came back without it.

After doing this for so long, I had to call him out on his actions. Richard insisted I was being paranoid, looking too far into the unimportant details and creating conspiracies in my head. The thing is, I know the definition of gaslighting. That's what he was doing – making me think I was going nuts and then continuing to do the thing he said he wasn't doing.

That's why I decided to check the barn for myself.

Richard caught me, of course. Just as I was sliding an arm into my coat, he happened to be coming out of his office for a cup of coffee, and his reddening cheeks gave him away. The suspicions I had about him having a secret were all but confirmed to me right then.

'Where are you going?' he asked.
'Out,' I told him smugly. 'Into the garden.'
'Why?'
'Well, I thought I might go clear out the barn.'
'Don't—'
'You can't stop me, dear husband.'
His panic was obvious, and I savoured every

second of it while I slipped on my shoes and went for the door. Richard tried to stop me, which only made me more suspicious, so I stormed towards the door to solve this mystery once and for all. Only, before I got there, he managed to stop me with one simple sentence.

'I'm making a gift for you! It's supposed to be a surprise!'

The comment stunned me into silence. Richard used to make me things all the time, but that's dwindled in recent years. Maybe he was falling out of love with me. But now that he was doing it again, I couldn't help hoping it was true.

'A surprise?' I said. 'What kind of a surprise?'

'It wouldn't be much of a surprise if I told you.'

'Well, is it in here?'

'No, actually,' he said after a long pause. 'It's in the woods. Not far from the well.'

'What?' I squinted at him, panicking. 'You went near the well?'

'Yes, why?'

'No reason.'

'No? Maybe I should go and take a look, then.'

As Richard started walking towards where I'd killed Emma, I took pursuit and tried to stop him. He got way too close, and a vision of my alternative futures started to flicker in my mind. It was basically prison, death, or death in prison. Those were my options.

Unless...

'Wait,' I snapped, stopping right in front of him. 'Let's make a deal. I won't ask any more questions about the surprise you have for me. In return, you stay away from the well. Because maybe, just *maybe*, I'm arranging a kind of surprise just like you are.'

Richard looked down on me, reading my reaction. It really felt as though he'd see right through it, push me aside, and have the police there within minutes. It would have been to his detriment, but at that point, he would probably have gone through with it anyway.

'Okay,' he said, which almost bowled me over. 'Let's get back in the warmth, then.'

I didn't hesitate to follow his lead, and to be honest, I'd already forgotten about whatever gift he was planning to make for me. I was too busy feeling grateful that he didn't find Emma's corpse, which was sure to have started the decomposing process by then. In short, I got lucky.

But my luck wouldn't last forever.

. . .

ONLY ONE DAY LATER, I was on my hands and knees in one of the upstairs showers when I heard voices. I remember stopping because it was so unusual in this house – Richard always stayed in his office, barely having any communication with his own son, and yet I could distinctly hear the two of them talking in a low whisper.

I dropped my sponge and Dettol bottle, tore off my gloves, and crept down the hall to Jacob's bedroom. There was a slight creak of the floorboards while I tiptoed, but not much. I made it all the way to our son's door and overheard the conversation clear as day.

'But I don't *want* to stay,' Jacob whined.

'We have to, buddy,' Richard said calmly, smoothly, in the deep, relaxing tone of his. 'At least for a while longer. Your mother is going through a hard time, and she's unwell, but she'll get better. Then, maybe we can get a fresh start.'

'You mean in a different house?'

'Perhaps. Is that something you want?'

'Okay, but...'

'What is it?'

'If I stay, do you promise not to hurt me?'

Heat flushed right through me then. It was like naked flames were licking up at my skull. Richard was just getting his first clue that I'd been turning his son against him. All the stuff I'd told him – about his father's temper, how much he liked to hit, and even that Richard didn't like his own son – were just about to come to the surface. I could just picture my darling husband inside that room then, on one knee with a twisted frown, hoping to dig a little deeper. He was clueless as to what had happened, but he was about to figure it all out.

I had to stop him.

'Jacob,' I said, entering the room. As best I could, I occupied the doorway and gave him a stern look, letting him know not to say any more. 'Isn't it about time you went and had a snack? Try the cupboard left of the oven. You might find something nice there.'

Without even an ounce of excitement, Jacob climbed up from his knees, brushed right past my legs, then went downstairs out of the way. Richard didn't move – he only continued to kneel there, looking up at me disapprovingly.

'What?' I challenged him.

'Why does our son think I'd hurt him?'

'No idea. Kids are weird.'

'He's six, Nora. He shouldn't even know me hurting him is possible.'

I shrugged, trying to act like I wasn't that interested in the conversation. 'Like I said, kids are weird. Now, are you done trying to find problems where there aren't any, or can I go and continue cleaning our home for the fifty millionth time?'

Richard shook his head in disgust, so I didn't wait for an answer. I simply turned and left, making my way back to the bathroom, where I'd resume my duties. I must admit, I was starting to wonder if there was even any point, given that a new idea had popped into my head. Upon realising that Richard was going to start the process of driving a wedge between me and my son, it became shockingly apparent that things were about to take a turn for the worse.

So I stewed on it for hours. Maybe even a day or two. However long it took, I remember standing at the end of the hall and looking at Richard's office on the far end. The door was open, and he was clattering china in the kitchen. This was my chance, I realised that night. It was my chance to take back control of how our story would end.

I would start by taking that rifle from the wall.

. . .

THE RIFLE FELT right in my hands. The weight sat in my arms as if it were made to be there. Richard seemed to think he had some antique on the wall, but he was dead wrong. How did I know this? Let's just say my father liked guns, and I'd never told my husband because I didn't want to emasculate him. This was back when I hadn't learned to punish him, of course.

Something else to know about this particular rifle was that it was a two-shooter. It was capable of holding two rounds at once – no more, no less. I checked it was loaded, then, satisfied, decided I'd have to deal with Richard first, then Jacob. That would make it all a lot easier. As for myself... I'd have to find a different way. Something without pain, unlike falling down a well or what happened to Katie. I even considered an overdose. Then we could all be together again, in a magical place up in the sky without cold weather, illnesses, pain, and...

Tutors.

'Whoa. What are you doing?'

At the sound of Richard's voice, I spun around and raised the rifle, taking aim. His eyes shot open like he'd just been splashed with ice water, and he raised his hands. For a moment, it looked like he was about to bolt through the door. We couldn't have that.

'Come inside and stand against the wall,' I said.

'Be careful, Nora. That thing's loaded.'

'You don't think I know that? Wall – *now*.'

Richard seemed reluctant, like he was trying to figure out if I was serious. The truth is, I'd never been more serious in all my life. Not that obeying my order would save his life, but it would at least save me the stress of chasing him through the house. It also eliminated the risk of him getting Jacob to safety. The kid was next, after all.

After a painfully long pause, Richard moved across the room with his hands still up. When he reached the corner, he bent his finger just enough to point at the rifle that was trained on him. 'That's not a toy, you know.'

'I know. But I want *you* to know that I really wanted us to work. I would have done anything for you – *anything* – and all you ever did was throw it back in my face. You don't have a clue how to treat a woman, do you?'

'What the...?' Richard scowled and shook his head. 'I might have stopped taking you on holidays for a while, but we had a kid together. It got harder. Work puts a lot of pressure on me, and it's hard to be this man. If that made you feel less than special... I'm sorry.'

'It's too late for apologies. What I wanted was for you to change.'

'I'm not a bad person, Nora. You know that.'

'Sure I do, but the people of Wedchester have been hearing their own version.'

Richard sagged in the middle as he lowered his hands, sadness making his face droop. It's funny, he genuinely believed he was a good man because... what? He worked really hard and provided for us? That wasn't enough for me. I'd wanted him to be a husband *and* a father, *and* the worker, *and* the housecleaner. I'd even wanted a dog so that lazy little bastard could walk it and know what it's like to have everything on his shoulders. But I'd barely got any of that, and any woman would agree I deserved it all.

They didn't have to know I'd been lying about him since day one.

In fact, I'd been lying about everything. How else could I get them on my side?

'Just because we spent some time together,' I said calmly, 'I'm going to allow you to get on your knees and tell me how much you want to live.

Believe me, my hope that you'll actually do this is the only thing keeping you alive.'

Richard scoffed. 'I would rather die like a man than a dog.'

'To me, they're one and the same thing. Fun for a while, then—'

'You're sick, Nora. You need help.'

'Help is for the living. The three of us? We're doing our own thing.'

'You mean...?'

As Richard took a brave step forward, I stepped back and tightened my grip on the rifle. If he moved again, he was going to take a rifle blast to the chest. It'd been a while since I'd fired one of these things and the recoil might have knocked me back, but my aim should have been true enough at that range. I always was a good shot. That's what Daddy always said.

'You're not going to hurt Jacob,' he said. 'I won't allow that.'

'I'm the one calling the shots, thank you. Now, on your knees.'

What happened next was one of those blink-and-you'll-miss-it events that changes your entire life. Richard lunged forward, hate lighting up his eyes like a furnace. My heart felt like it stopped for half a second while I held my breath and took aim. As predicted, I got shoved onto my back leg when I squeezed the trigger. The rifle shot exploded through the house. By the time this was done, I knew life would never be the same.

Richard had already hit the floor, motionless as he lay in a pool of his own blood. I stood there over his dead body, even kicking it twice to make sure he was really gone. Should I have felt sadness then or joy at the fact that the hardest part of tonight's work was done? Prescribing the same fate to Jacob wasn't going to be hard.

All I had to do was find him.

Chapter Twenty-Six

My feet don't move at first. It's like it's freezing again, my heels rooted to the ground in ice. More ice seizes my back, making me shiver from head to toe. Somewhere deep in my mind is a weaker, more cowardly version of me trying to convince me not to go back into that house.

'Emma,' it says. *'You've got your life. Keep it by running away!'*

Just like all cowards, I'm inclined to listen to it. Running or hiding is always the easiest option at the time but the hardest to live with. I turn around and look back at the gates – past them, where Wedchester sits in a canvas of black with its pub lights and bedroom lamps lighting it up like stars. It seems like such a peaceful place where nothing could ever hurt you. It is an option, I tell myself, but behind me...

I look up at the house. That was definitely a gunshot, and only two people could have reached it, much less fired it. Taking into account everything Richard ever said, I doubt it was him. And if Nora has already hurt Jacob...

My stomach knots with worry. That poor little guy never deserved anything but the best. Even Richard, who started as my enemy and later became my friend, deserves to be rescued. He's a good guy, and his care for my well-being pretty much cements that I owe him.

'But what if he's tricked you just like Nora did?' my little coward asks.

No, I'm trying to get out of it. There's nothing about this situation that could let me walk away. Whoever it is that needs my help, it's my responsibility to get inside and help them right now. There's not enough time to run back to town, which pretty much leaves one choice.

Despite my paralysing fear, I must force myself to move.

Before I can stop myself, I run for the house.

I just hope it's not too late.

. . .

I ENTER through the back door where Nora used to smoke. It's the only one that's unlocked, but the lights inside are off. I can't see five feet in front of me, so I'm extremely careful as I make my way past the kitchen island. The only thing I can see is my fogged breath expelling in front of me, an aftermath of my time out in the cold.

Soon, my hands bump into something hard and flat. I feel around the door for its handle, pull the damn squeaky thing gently, and then let go of my breath as light from the hallway floods the kitchen. The whole time, I'm haunted by the threatening image of Nora standing there with that rifle pointed at my face, ready to take the shot and do what she always wanted.

To kill me, not just the once but for a second time.

I don't know where to go or who to look for. Hearing a gunshot is one thing, but until I see confirmation of who fired and who it hit, I have to assume any of the possibilities are true. That's why I take my time stepping into the hallway, slowly peering around the corner and gawking up at the massive staircase. The lights in here are on, and I can hear the faint patter of footsteps coming from somewhere in the house. The problem is they could be coming from literally anywhere on either floor, so there's no guaranteed safe spot.

Fear might be a factor in this, but I decide to wait it out. Nora won't find me here unless she specifically wants to use the kitchen. This gives me a little time – not much, but a little – to pray for Jacob and his father. They're both good people who deserve the happily ever after. Although my heart bleeds to even contemplate that what they'll get is the complete opposite.

Damn you, Nora.

I don't even know what I'll do if I run into her. She might have a rifle, but even if she doesn't, I'm hardly a match for her. I never was a fighter, even when it really mattered. I remember a boy pushing himself onto me at a house party when I was younger. I was a brave drunk – maybe even a little bitchy – but I wasn't brave enough to do much more than tell him no. Thankfully, my sister and friends were there to rip him off me. They went a step further, too: they publicly shamed him and had him expelled from school.

Good riddance.

Finally, I hear a voice in the distance. Torn away from my painful memory, I step over to the corner and peer around it again, straining to listen.

It takes a while to come again, but when it does, I recognise the cruel, maniacal voice all over again. The voice of a killer.

I clutch my stomach, a sinking pain setting in at the thought of that six-year-old delight being murdered by his own mother. Panic takes over my body, my breath coming in short, desperate rasps as tears breach my eyes. I wipe them away and breathe deeply, steadily.

Then, the voice comes again.

'Jacob,' Nora says as if to summon him. 'Darling, come out here. I won't hurt you.'

I don't know what to feel exactly, but the very fact she's calling out to him tells me two things: Jacob is still alive, and Richard probably isn't. There's no way he would allow Nora to get this close – to stalk through the house like a hunter seeking her prey.

'Come to Mummy,' she says. 'I'll get you some Pop-Tarts. Does that sound good?'

It goes to show how well she knows her own son. Jacob hates Pop-Tarts, and even he wouldn't be stupid enough to fall for that anyway. I thank God for Nora's bad choice of bribes as I see a long shadow stretch out across the upstairs wall. It's long and slender and holding a rifle in its hands.

Then the shadow gets smaller, and Nora's body comes into focus on the landing, scanning the main hall like a murder drone.

That's when I shrink back and let her walk around.

'I'm starting to get very angry at you,' she shouts down the stairs. 'If you come out now, Mummy will forgive you. But if you don't and I find you, there will be a very severe punishment. Just do the right thing, young man.'

Nora waits. I wait, imagining how scared that little boy must be.

Seconds later, those footsteps pad down the stairs. I hold my breath and press my back to the wall while she comes into view. This is it – the very last moment of my life – and all I've got to show for my years on this Earth is a suitcase full of worthless possessions.

Just like Katie.

Nora turns then, skulking down the hall with that damn rifle back in her hands. A memory comes back to me while I watch her leave: Richard telling me it only holds two rounds. She's already used one – I don't want to imagine what damage she caused with that – which means she only has the power to take one more life tonight.

I'll just be happy if it's not Jacob's.

Now that her back is turned and I know she's downstairs, I hurry up the steps and start searching for him. I don't try his bedroom just yet, figuring that Nora probably went there first and didn't find him. Wherever he is, he's surely too scared to move without guidance. That's why I start whispering to him, calling out as I head down the hall while pushing open doors. Some of these rooms are familiar to me, but some are brand new. The billiards room, for example, I didn't even know was there until just now.

These people are way too rich.

'Jacob,' I keep trying, whispering every time I push open a door. 'It's me, Emma. You need to come out so we can get away from here, okay? I'll protect you. You'll be safe.'

That's the lie I tell, anyway. Realistically, I have no bloody idea what to do when he finally reveals himself. Run, I suppose, but Nora isn't stupid. She'll have the doors covered, and a rifle round can move a hell of a lot faster than me.

When I reach the end of the corridor, I'm about to give up. Nora is still calling for her son downstairs, and I'm as clueless as she is. It's time I start looking for Richard, and I'm about to do just that when I hear a snivelling whimper from somewhere in the gymnasium.

'Jacob?' I say gently. 'Is that you?'

He doesn't say anything, but his tears give him away. I go inside, thinking how much I'd be rolling my eyes at the expensive, probably unused gym equipment in here. Following the sounds of youthful sniffles, I find Jacob hiding behind a stack of safety mats that are propped up against the wall. He has his knees to his chest and his face buried in his folded arms.

'Hey, it's me,' I tell him, softly putting a hand on his arm. 'It's Emma.'

'Mummy is trying to hurt me,' he whines. 'She k-killed Daddy.'

My knees go weak at the sound of those words, but Richard is gone. We can mourn him later, but right now, we need to get the hell out of here. There's no time like the present, so I take Jacob's hand and encourage him out of his hiding spot. When I start to move, he tugs at my top and then opens his arms. I didn't expect to have to carry him out of here, but I'll do whatever it takes to keep him safe.

After all, I'm all he has now.

Scooping him into my arms, I rush back into

the hall and make a beeline for the stairs. As soon as we get there, Nora appears from one of the downstairs doors. Sweat rolling down my temple, I turn and look back where we came from. All those doors are open and inviting, but there's no time to reach them. Instead, I tear open the nearest one and head inside, closing it behind us and locking us inside the cramped, dark laundry cupboard.

That's where we wait to die.

Jacob clings to me. There's a thin bar of light under the door. The silhouette of feet comes and go as Nora haunts the upper floor with her husband's rifle. Whenever Jacob starts to sob, I cover his mouth and hold him closer. It will take a bullet to make me let him go.

I'll probably get that bullet, too.

Over time, Nora's constant back and forth becomes slower. She goes for a long period of time, but I'm too scared to make a run for it. It's only a matter of time until she checks this cupboard, but what if we dare to step out of it and run for the stairs? What if she's out there waiting for us, that trigger finger of hers dangerously itchy?

That's how Richard suffered, wasn't it?

I think back to the gunshot I heard. Perhaps there's a chance she missed – that he's somewhere in the house, looking for Jacob just like I was. It's naïve and stupid to hope for such a thing, but when you're stuck inside a dark room and holding a child as you both wait for death, it's those little thoughts that keep you going.

Jacob needs it, too. He hasn't let go of my coat since we got in here, gripping it fiercely like his life depends on it. After a while, he gazes up at me with his teary eyes sparkling. His bottom lip is quivering, and I hold him close as if to answer the question he just asked me with his eyes. Words simply aren't necessary, but I know what he wants.

A promise that he'll make it out of here alive.

The problem is I don't want to lie to him.

Chapter Twenty-Seven

A WHOLE LIFETIME passes inside that cupboard. A long, arduous one full of pain and suffering. Jacob hasn't left my side after all this time – he's as scared as I am. The difference is I'm not allowed to let it show. The boy's mother has finally gone over the edge, and his father is dead. It does leave me to wonder, even if we make it out of here alive, what will happen to him?

At least the footsteps have slowly gone away. We still hear Nora shuffle back and forth occasionally, but not as intensely as a few minutes ago. As she stalks up and down the hallways, she reminds me of Jack Nicholson in *The Shining*. You just need to swap out the rifle for an axe and the messy blonde hair for a prematurely balding head.

The next time those footsteps come and go, Jacob takes his head away from my shoulder, where he's been stuck to me like glue. Using his sleeve, he wipes at his eyes and sniffs deeply. Then, quietly, he asks, 'What are we going to do?'

I shake my head. 'We'll need to make a run for it, but we can't go too soon.'

'I don't want to be here. Please can we go?'

'Not yet, sweetie. Soon, okay?'

'Why is she trying to...?' The rest of the question speaks for itself, but it's too much for a six-year-old to process. His head droops back down, and then he puts his head back on my shoulder and clutches my coat tighter.

I wish there was something I could do. This is the sorriest I've felt for anyone, and that includes Nora (back when I thought she was a half-decent human being). I don't have kids of my own – never really thought about having any either – but there's a maternal instinct that seems to have kicked in with Jacob. When, or indeed *if*, we get out of here, there's nothing I want more than to ensure he goes to a good home. And I know that makes him sound like an unwanted puppy, but you understand.

A short while later, when I was just starting to talk myself into running, the footsteps return. That cold shiver rattles down my spine once again. The light under the door blinks out as Nora slowly passes. Jacob holds me close, and I hold him back.

'Please don't let her get me,' he says in a quiet whimper.

The footsteps stop. I clap a hand over Jacob's mouth. The shadow glides along the carpet, making its way back to us. My body tenses up. I hold Jacob tight, pivoting him around as if to shield him while the shuffling stops outside. The bar of light is gone. Nora is standing right outside the door, and Jacob starts to sob in my arms. I wish I could make him quieter – to end his tears and suffering – but a few seconds from now, we could both be dead.

The door handle creaks. We sit there in the dark. Time slows down while I watch the handle lower. I want to rush forward and hold it – force it to stay shut – but I'm frozen with terror and cannot move. Even to save my life. Even to save Jacob.

Then, the door springs open. Light explodes into the room. Jacob cries harder and buries himself behind me. I shut my eyes tight and await the rifle blast that will end it all. And while I sit there awaiting death, I have just enough time to pray that the round won't go right through me. All I want is for this kid to be safe.

Even if it means me dying.

'There you are,' Nora says with spite in her voice.

I don't so much as look up at her because I'm too afraid. All I can do is shield my eyes and scrunch them up tight to accept the death that's coming. Only it seems to be taking forever, and in that long, dreadful silence, I realise the spite in her voice isn't spite at all but the desperate sucking of air from a wounded person. And that voice I hear – Nora's voice – isn't Nora's at all. It's deeper than that.

It's Richard's.

'Emma?' he says. 'Jacob?'

Jacob looks up just as I do. There he is, standing in the doorway in hunched, twisted agony with blood coating his entire torso. One hand is clutched to his shoulder, and he's leaning against the door just to stay upright. It's a pale imitation of the strong, intimidating man I once knew, but he's in there somewhere. Under all the blood, there's Richard.

Without so much as a word, Jacob lets go of me and climbs to his feet. He runs to his father and hugs him tight, blood sticking to his clothes. I watch the reunion with my heart throbbing. There's a certain sweetness to how little either one of them cares about the smearing blood – it's like nothing else exists in this moment except for the two of them.

It's beautiful.

'Are either of you hurt?' Richard asks, aiming the question at me.

'No, but you are.'

'Yes... we need to move fast.'

Richard's hard stare at me tells me what he's trying to say: the gunshot wound is severe, and the blood loss even more so. It's only a matter of time until he takes his last breath, so we need to get out of here while his heart is still beating. He can't say that in front of his son, of course, but that's what the subtext reads.

I'm not about to waste any more time, so I rush to my feet and pull Jacob away from his father. There's no resistance – he holds my hand and gets blood everywhere – but he's coming without a single argument. I look to Richard for help as he knows this house better than me.

'She locked the front door,' he says. 'I don't know where the key is.'

'The back door is open,' I tell him. 'It's how I got inside.'

'Then that's where we're going.'

With my free arm, I help support Richard as we leave the hallway. It's so bright up here (was it always this bright?), but it's better than being too dark. If Nora comes running around a corner, then I want to spot her way ahead of time. We'll need every advantage we can get.

After hobbling down the stairs, Richard stops and then starts to sway. I help hold him upright, but he puts up a hand as if telling me to give him space. Jacob and I both step away while he adjusts to the exertion, steadies himself, then nods.

'I'm okay,' he says. 'Let's—'

'Die?'

It's Nora's voice. I jump out of my skin and spin around. Jacob gasps, and Richard stumbles forward to step between us and the gun. My breath comes out in a weak, pathetic little draught as my mind hurries to put it all together: Nora has the rifle, and it's aimed at me, Richard's wound won't let him stay upright for much longer, and our only chance of escape?

It's through the door Nora is blocking.

THERE'S ONLY one round left in that gun.

You'd think that makes me feel at least a little safer, but it doesn't. The current situation is that Richard will die sometime very soon, and the last bullet will either kill me or Jacob. That's not to say she doesn't have spare ammunition, but I don't recall seeing any on the wall.

Got to appreciate the little things.

Nora's eyes land on me, widening with shock in the stressfully quiet hall. All I can hear is everyone's deep, laboured breathing and the persistent tick-tock of that godawful grandfather clock. Nora's hands twitch as if to raise the gun at me, but she seems to think better of it.

'You're supposed to be dead,' she says begrudgingly.

'Sorry to disappoint.' I can't stop looking at that rifle.

'I suppose this is what you were doing in that barn?' Nora asks Richard, turning the gun on him. He wants to rush her – I can see it in the way his leg inches forward – but he thinks better of it. It looks like being on the brink of death hasn't affected his good sense.

'I was trying to help a woman in need.'

'Shame you couldn't extend that same courtesy to Katie.'

'That wasn't supposed to happen. You know that.'

'Yeah, well, it did.' Nora aims down her sight. 'Now, why don't you save us all a lot of time and step aside? There's a bullet in here with that young man's name on it.'

Richard turns his head just a little, side-eyeing me. I know what he wants and act accordingly. Putting a hand on Jacob's shoulder, I move in front of him and act as body armour. If Nora absolutely has to fire that gun, she'll have to use it on me or Richard first.

There's no way we'll let her kill a child.

'Put the gun down,' Richard says with a restrained, calm voice. 'This isn't right.'

'Not the way you see it, sure.' Nora scoffs. 'But things are messed up beyond all repair. Our marriage is a wreck, and our son likes his tutors more than his own mother. There's no way to recover from this. Not in life, at any rate.'

'Is that what all this is about? The destruction of our family?'

'It's not about the death. I'm all about the rebirth.'

Richard shakes his head, and I look at the door behind Nora. It would be impossible to get there without knocking her down. Or, at the very least, talking her away from it. I crane my neck towards the stairs, considering making a run for it. There's no way out up there, but at least we could lure her away from the door and try again.

'Why don't you just put the gun down?' Richard says, swaying again. 'We can talk this through, maybe even get counselling. Listen to me. I'll do whatever it takes to bring our marriage back to what it used to be. It will take work, but we can do it. Together.'

Nora scoffs again, but the gears are turning behind her eyes. Is he tricking her, or is he deadly serious? After everything I've seen and heard, it's hard to believe he would really give her another shot. And that's if – 'if' being the operative word – he makes it through the night. I wonder, if I manage to run for an ambulance now, will Richard survive?

'Did you really think I'd fall for that?' Nora asks, grinning.

'It's not a trick.' Richard sways so hard he has to put his hand against the wall just to stay upright. A red smear drags out from under his palm. He hisses at the pain but perseveres. It's amazing what a father's love can do. 'Look, things have got out of hand, but that doesn't mean we can't fix this. All it's going to take is for you to put the gun down.'

'You must think I'm stupid.'

'Nora, I don't—'

'Spare me the bullshit, will you? I've got things to do.'

As quickly as that, she steps to one side and takes aim at Jacob. I'm still in the way, and Nora's frustration shows through her gritted teeth. My breath leaves me with a wheeze as I fear for my life, but Richard intercepts. He lashes out and grabs the gun weakly, giving us an extra few seconds to live.

Or to run.

'Go!' he screams at me with what little life he has left. 'Get Jacob out of here!'

In his current bloodied, near-death state, Nora is stronger than him. Richard screams through the pain of his gunshot wound and wrestles for the rifle. I stand there, frozen, tempted to dart forward and help him, but that would leave Jacob vulnerable.

When I recover my senses, snapping back to the moment, it's clear what I must do. Without wasting so much as a single second, I turn, sweep Jacob up into my arms, and run up the stairs as fast as I can. It's not until I reach the top that I turn long enough to see Richard – his body now motionless on the floor as Nora stares up at us.

Then, I realise what we've done.

We've just left him to die.

Chapter Twenty-Eight

This is what they call fight or flight mode. Richard's death will hit me later, but right now, we're right back where we were a few minutes ago. Only this time, Nora knows we're both up here, and Jacob is a trembling mess in my arms.

It doesn't even register how heavy he is until we're halfway down the hall. I'm out of breath, sweating, feeding off pure adrenaline just to keep us both alive. Richard trusted me to keep his kid safe, and I'll do whatever it takes to make that happen.

Whatever it takes.

When we reach the end of the hall, we're officially out of options. I turn just long enough to see Nora reach the top of the stairs. That damn rifle is still in her hands, and she takes aim at us. Before she can take her shot, I dash into the nearest room and slam the door shut.

'She's coming,' Jacob says in a hurried breath.

I pay no attention to him, setting him down and feeling around the darkness for a door bolt. Eventually, my shaking hands find a light switch, revealing there's no lock of any kind. I've seen plenty of films where people are getting chased through a house, so I don't hesitate to grab a nearby chair. It wedges firmly between the door handle and the floor.

In a roundabout sort of way, the door is locked. For now.

With a minute left to catch my breath, I encourage Jacob away from the door. Nora is pounding on it now, the wooden thudding sounding like thunderous dog barks. Jacob is still crying as I look around the room for something to fight with. I didn't even realise there was a box room in this house – everything else has been so perfectly decorated that I assumed Nora didn't want to leave a room looking messy and disused.

Which explains why it's at the end of the hall.

The knocking continues. Nora shouts through the door, something about shooting if I don't open up. I know – or at least I *hope* – she only has one bullet left, so she's free to waste it firing into thin air. I just pray it doesn't catch one of us by dumb luck.

'Emma, open this door right this instant and I might spare your life!'

No chance, I think, then start rummaging through the boxes.

Jacob appears at my side, ripping open the damp cardboard at an equally hurried pace. 'What should I look for?' he asks. 'A gun?'

'I doubt we'll find a gun. Just something hard that I can fight with.'

'Will you hurt my mummy?'

'Yes, of cour...' I stop to look down at him, worry completing his look of utter devastation. Even after all that's happened, he doesn't want his mother to get hurt. I find it astonishing that he would have so much care for someone who's trying to kill him.

I have no such care.

With fighting out of the question, there's only one thing left to do. I run to the window and take a peek outside. There's a sloped roof that might hold us, as long as the tiles aren't too icy. My heart is racing at the sound of the chair screeching behind me. It won't hold forever, but I think we might be able to climb onto the garage roof if we're lucky.

If we're *quick*.

I slide open the window, but by then, all hope is lost. The chair gives way. The door swings open so hard it slams against the wall. Nora is standing in the opening, the rifle held firmly in her hands as I grab Jacob and stand with him behind me once more. Meanwhile, the freezing wind is blowing at my back, taunting me to take my chances.

At this point, anything can happen.

'Get out of the way, Emma.' Nora steps forward, her stance militant. I know nothing about guns, but it looks like she knows what she's doing. Her dead husband is evidence of that. 'You don't have to die, as long as you just step aside and make this easy.'

I'm no mother, but I'll never understand how someone can let harm come to her child. Much less *bring* the harm to them. Even as a recent addition to Jacob's life, I'll give my own life to protect him. That part is non-negotiable. Not as his tutor, but as a person.

I reach my hands behind me to make sure he's still there.

'You're not getting to him,' I say, looking Nora in the eye – looking death in the face.

'Don't you understand? I have to.'

'Why?'

'Because happiness doesn't exist in this world.'

Something about that phrasing takes me aback. Nora talks as though this is the only option – like she was always destined to do this. But it's not just her take on the current situation that scares me. Her own husband is dead, and it's all because of her, but there's not a single sign of remorse. Nothing about her even remotely suggests she regrets it.

There don't seem to be any emotions whatsoever.

'You can be happy,' I tell her, appealing to her more desperate, depressed side. 'With or without Richard, you'll always have Jacob. You'll get some inheritance from Richard, I'm guessing? Maybe even all of it?'

Nora lowers the gun by just an inch, then gives a short, sharp nod.

'Then you can start rebuilding, no?'

'But Richard... I'll go to prison.'

'Nobody has to know what happened here tonight.'

Nora seems to consider this. I turn my head just enough to check on Jacob. He's still quivering behind me, but he subtly points to the window like he wants to climb through it. I wish I could be that brave – to *want* to climb out there and make a run for it.

I nod, mouthing, 'In a minute.'

Then I realise what I've done. In less than thirty seconds, I've convinced Nora that she can live happily ever after, taking Jacob with her and keeping her evil deeds buried in the past. Just as I remind myself she has one bullet left, it finally clicks that I've offered her a way out at my own expense – that I'm the only one who knows the whole truth.

That the past will be buried with me.

I step back, my shaky breath falling out of my mouth in a weird, stuttering sound. Nora shuffles forward a few inches, the rifle still trained on me. She casts a quick glance to my side, and I feel the break in the wind as Jacob slowly climbs out onto the roof. There's a limited window for her to make a split decision, and I'm scared the urgency will push her into doing something stupid – something dangerous.

'You're the last one who knows,' she says, catching on to my mistake.

'Nora. Please don't—'

'I want you to know it was never personal. The well... what happens next...'

The pounding of my heart feels like a dance track, my mouth dry and my legs trembling. The only mercy is the cold blowing in through the open window, chilling the sweat on my back. I swallow hard, checking over my shoulder once more to find Jacob has made it fully onto the roof. There's room for me out there, as long as I can move fast enough.

This is it now. The one swift, daring motion as I leap towards the window. Before Nora can come closer, I steel myself for what's about to happen. The window is free, her aim fixed on me, and I finally do what needs to be done.

I take the leap.

IN THE RACE for my life, I climb out onto the roof. There's a voice behind me, shrill and desperate as it barks at me to get back inside and take what's coming to me. Obeying that order would mean certain death, so I take my chances in the freezing open air.

The wind whips at my head. I find Jacob on the tiles next to me, his fragile little six-year-old fingers grasping onto the guttering for dear life. I take his hands and tell him to trust me – that it's all going to be okay if only he will let me take care of him.

Yes, I lie to him.

Behind us, Nora's shadow occupies the window, the rifle unable to reach us because of the obscured angle. We're not safe here – we could die at any moment, if not from a gunshot, then from the fall. The ground below, although grassy and moist from the melted snow, is so far away that the fall is likely to kill us. But it's still safer than staying up here with Nora.

This can only mean one thing.

We have to jump.

I lead Jacob towards the end of the roof, standing behind him and watching his balance. He fully trusts me to lead him there safely, the icy wind taking our breath away. When we reach the edge, there's a long leap to the nearest low roof of the garage. I stand there, sweating despite the cold, measuring the distance with nothing but sight. My heart sinks when I realise.

I'm not sure we can make it.

'Do we have to jump?' Jacob whines over the fierce, night-time wind.

'Maybe.'

Glancing back at the window, I can only see the rifle perched over the edge. It's clear what she's doing now: she's watching the main gate and patiently awaiting her chance to kill me from afar. It's great that there's no room for her to pivot the weapon, but as soon as we make it down to the ground – *if* we make it down – there's still that to contend with.

'All right,' I tell Jacob, slowly kneeling to meet his beady, vulnerable little eyes. I understand his fear because I feel it myself. Even more than the harsh, unforgiving cold of this ice-cold night, the terror is seeping into my bones. 'Here's what we're going to do. You see that outcropping over the garage roof?'

Jacob's terrified gaze drifts over to the ledge far below us. 'Yeah...'

'I'm going to jump over there. When I get across, you're going to have to jump.'

'But—'

'You have to, sweetie. It's the only way out.'

'What if I fall?'

'I'll catch you.'

'Promise?'

'I promise.'

Nora is still at the window, the rifle waiting for us when we try to get out of here. I'll worry about that in a minute because right now, my main concern is getting us onto the ground without breaking every bone in our bodies. I turn to look at the garage roof and, knowing there's no room behind me for a run-up, take a deep breath.

Then jump.

The freezing air cuts through me, a drift of wind lashing up at my numb cheeks while I close the gap. The roof races up to meet me, the hard tile slicing the skin on my leg. I let out an exhilarated breath, grateful to have made it in spite of the damage it did to my leg. There's no time to worry about grazes and cuts – we might not survive the next few minutes.

'Okay, Jacob,' I scream over the wind. 'It's your turn. Come on.'

'I'm scared,' he calls back, peering over the edge.

'Don't look down there. Just look at me, okay. Right here.'

Jacob stares into my eyes, his bottom lip still shaking.

'You can do this,' I say, desperate to instil confidence.

'I can't.'

'Yes, you can. Trust me!'

While Jacob sizes up the gap again, I take one more look at Nora. The rifle hasn't moved, and her hands are so steady on that weapon. I'm starting to think she's a very confident shooter, which doesn't provide a whole lot of hope for getting out of here alive. I'm trying to look on the bright side though: at least she hasn't run downstairs to stop us.

'Okay,' Jacob shouts, finally finding his inner strength. 'Are you ready?'

'Yes.'

I have to bury my doubts. Shifting as close as I can to the edge of the roof, I hold out my arms and get ready to catch him. Jacob – still a child, I must remind myself – shifts his weight to the back foot. His tiny chest rises as he takes a deep breath.

Then, putting all his faith in me, he jumps.

Chapter Twenty-Nine

Jacob misses.

It's not that surprising, given how little his legs are. It's a big jump that even I barely made, but the last thing I wanted to do was make him doubt the jump. The thing is, if he didn't jump, then Nora would likely have waited for him to come inside and then taken the shot.

After all, if she couldn't kill me, then she only had one other option.

My hand wraps around Jacob's. My balance betrays me. I fall forward, his weight tugging me down. My entire body collapses and strikes the roof. A tile slides out from under me, then shatters as it strikes a small patch of concrete below.

'Emma!' he screams above the howling wind.

'Hold on!'

It takes every ounce of my strength to heave him onto the roof. His little voice is like a screeching in my ear as I pull him into my arms, falling back with him on top of me. I hold him close while he squeezes against me like I'm the only thing left in his world.

Which is true.

We're safe then, but not for long. Nora's rifle is still visible in the window, and somehow, we have to get off the garage roof. I climb to my feet, begging Jacob to uncoil his little arms from around my neck. He does so when he realises there's no other choice, which gives me time to figure out how to get down.

Richard's Jaguar is down below. It's not too big a drop, and under different circumstances, I might feel bad about landing on an expensive sports car. I guess it's not like he'll miss it – Richard is dead, so his care for material things is long gone.

I tell Jacob to wait, then begin my descent to the car. It's a short gap that is of no challenge at all after what we just went through. Even Jacob seems to approach this one with ease, knowing I'll catch him even if he does somehow slip and fall.

My first bit of real luck occurs when Jacob

lands in my arms. I let out a sigh of relief and then hop off the Jaguar, almost slipping off the frost-slicked roof. After helping Jacob down, I stand on the corner of the house with him hugging my hips.

Now that we're safely on the ground, there's only one way out of here without risking our necks in the woods. I'm never going to try that again, so all I can do is get a good look at the distance from our position to the gates. It's not *too* far, and maybe we can make it.

But then what? Run down the hill and beg for help? It almost seems too easy, if only we can get through the gate. I am, however, reminded that Nora has taken a sniper's position up in the window, but I'm not sure how much of the front yard she can see from there.

I guess there's only one way to find out.

JACOB HOLDS MY HAND. I hold my breath. The next few seconds are going to make the difference between life and death. The young boy looks up at me, his horror buried deep beneath the surface of trust in his eyes. He sees me as his guardian, and I guess I am.

'Are you ready?' I ask.

Jacob nods, and that's all it takes. I grip his hand tightly and think happy thoughts – of how lucky we were to make it out of the house and onto the roof. I think about how unbelievably fortunate we were to jump from roof to roof with no injuries (save the gaping scratch on my leg). As I take those first steps that break into a run, I try not to think about getting shot but about luck finding us one last time and letting us pass the gate unharmed.

No such thing happens.

It's Nora's voice that stops me halfway between the house and the gate. It comes out of the darkness like a red flash of anger, filling my heart with dread. When I stop in my tracks, something tells me the well wasn't the only time she was going to kill me.

My good fortune has come to an end.

'Don't you dare move!' she yells from her perch on the window. 'If I want to, I can blow your head clean off at this range. Don't make me waste my last bullet, Emma. It wasn't meant for you. Just step aside and walk away.'

I shiver in the wind, looking down at the young boy, who only wants to live. Judging from what she just said, she doesn't currently have a clear shot at

Jacob. *Good*, I think. *Let's keep it that way and see if we can live a while longer.*

'You know I can't do that,' I call back, turning to gaze up at her. I'm careful not to step out of the line between Nora and her son. How good a marksman is she, exactly? Does she need much more than an inch of opportunity to take the kill shot on her son?

She scoffs so loud I hear it from down here. 'You're willing to trade your life for his?'

'If that's what it takes.'

'Then you're an idiot.'

'With all due respect, I'm not the one who just killed my husband.'

Nora shakes her head, but all I see is the silhouette. Any word might be my last, so I'm careful not to step too far. Dying without losing my sense of pride is one thing, but taunting her too far might push her over the edge. If she fires that gun, Jacob might be able to run away from her. I think Nora knows that, and that's the only thing keeping me alive.

'Emma,' Jacob says, never sounding more fragile.

'What is it?'

'I'm scared.'

'So am I,' I whisper. 'But just stay behind me, okay?'

Jacob might have nodded, but I can't see behind me. My eyes are trained on Nora, just like hers are trained on me. The wind picks up, a low murmur riding on its breath like a tide. It sounds strange at first, like the whispers of a hundred ghosts each trying to be heard over the other. When it grows a little louder, I turn towards the bottom of the hill.

That's when I see it.

There's a small gathering at the base. The outline of ten, maybe fifteen people, huddle at the bottom, some pointing up at the house as they talk amongst themselves. The wind carries their voices, but I can't make out what they're saying. Not that I need to – relief is flooding through me, and I can't help but smile. They must have heard the first gunshot, I decide, and now they're close enough to see what Nora is about to do.

Although, sadly, not close enough to stop it.

As they begin their ascent up the hill – foolishly brave though they might be – I turn back up to Nora and wonder how long I have left. That time pressure is all I have to bargain with. This is my last chance to make her change her mind so we can all walk away with our lives.

'Nora... please. Put the gun down and let us go.'

'There's no way that's happening.'

'Nobody else needs to die. Look, it's over.'

'There's still time.'

'For what?' This comes out in a desperate, frustrated cry. My hands are shaking, and it's not just because of the cold. My entire body has gone tense, and my impending death is to blame. 'Let me tell you, there is no way in hell you're going to shoot Jacob. If you shoot me, these people will know what you did, and you'll spend the rest of your life in prison. Is that really what you want?'

Nora stands up straight, still peering down the rifle's sights. 'If he lives, we can't be together,' she says, as if it makes any kind of sense. 'At least if he dies, then I die, and we can all be together in Heaven. Together... forever.'

Jesus, she really has lost it.

What kind of woman really believes that she can murder two people – three, if that's what happened to Katie – and still get to walk through the Pearly Gates? I want to remind her that murder is a sin, but a comment like that won't help my situation.

'Regardless,' I say. 'You're not going to hurt Jacob.'

'Then you're going to have to be the one to die.'

'Why, Nora? It's like I said, it's all over. Nobody needs to get hurt.'

'But you...' Her voice comes back full of tears. 'It would have been okay if not for you.'

I don't know exactly what she imagined I've done wrong – standing in the way of a dual homicide, accepting the affections of her son while protecting him from a seriously premature death – but I'm not going to suffer from her own mental illness. Not any more. Not after nearly dying down that well. It's only thanks to Richard I'm still alive, and we all know what happened to him. I just wish he lived long enough for me to thank him properly.

'Last chance,' Nora says. 'Stand aside.'

I take a quick glance back at the people of Wedchester. They're still coming up the hill, but they're too far to help. All I can do is turn back to Nora and, petrified of what's going to happen next, square up to her. 'Not a chance.'

'Then you've made your choice.'

Before she can take the shot, I spin around and

haul Jacob into my arms. Keeping him close to my chest, I sprint through the gate and take my chances getting down the hill. I don't know how long I'm going to last, but all that's left to do is run as fast as I can.

Run and pray.

SOMEHOW, we make it to the road. Jacob's breath is hot against my neck as he clings to me for dear life. Nora is far behind us, possibly still in the window, but I won't be slowing down to look. The best thing I can do right now is just keep running and hope for the best.

The road is still icy under my feet. Not much, but enough to scare me as I run the fastest I've ever run in my entire life. Down at the bottom of the hill, the townsfolk are still coming. Some of them are using torches or phone lights to illuminate their path. There's nothing they can do to save us – not without standing in the way of that rifle – but I want to make it to them anyway. Even if just so Jacob can go free. After all, I have very little to live for.

He has his whole life ahead of him.

As if by some miracle, the cherry red and ocean

blue lights from a police car flash in the night. The sky brightens with hope and promise. Somehow, I smile, excitement filling me as I start to laugh. 'We're going to be okay,' I tell Jacob, panting. 'We're going to be safe.'

It's hard to say exactly when the bullet hits me. It can't be true, but it seems like I feel it before the gunshot screams through the dark. I stop running, cold shooting through my stomach. Jacob hasn't let go – does he know what's happened?

All my energy floods through the wound. I drop to my knees, setting down Jacob as gently as possible. Gasps sound from the bottom of the hill as the police car comes closer, its siren screaming like an old crone. When I look down, Jacob backs away, and I see the blood.

That's the last thing I lay eyes on before the world becomes a blur.

Then, just after I manage to smile at the boy I saved, everything goes black.

Chapter Thirty

NORA

I heard him coming, but I didn't care.

All I wanted was to make her suffer for everything she'd done to me. If I'm completely honest, I wasn't even sure I could make the shot under the best circumstances. But there was a high wind to account for, Emma was a moving target, and my emotions were getting the better of me. I was a good shot, but I wasn't *that* good.

Very few people were.

It didn't help that Richard had somehow picked himself up from the floor for a second time. I knew I should have strangled the life out of him when I had the chance, but Emma and Jacob had been getting away. Put yourself in my position, try to understand how tense things were getting, and only then could you truly appreciate the situation.

Now, I was paying for it.

The door had slammed shut from the wind, but it was opening now. I took a quick look away from my sights just to confirm it. Richard was standing there, still swaying, even less steady on his feet than before. I didn't doubt for a second that – even though he was bleeding out – he still had the strength to knock me out if he really wanted to. I may have won the first time, but now I wasn't trying to fight him.

I was trying to kill Emma.

My father's lessons came back to me in a flash. First, we had to figure out the distance, then we'd allow for bullet drop from me to her. Then there was the wind, I guessed around fourteen kilometres per hour, based on the way it tugged on the tree branches. Even as Richard stumbled up behind me, I was slow and deliberate, taking in a deep breath before my shot.

Then, I squeezed the trigger.

The rifle kicked back. I let it go just as

Richard's hands slammed on my shoulders. He tore me away from the window and threw me onto my back. A shot of delicious pain roared up my spine while he stood there, chest heaving, eyes closing and opening in heavy blinks. He thought he'd won, but he hadn't.

Because before he tossed me aside, I managed to see the damage I caused.

I got to see the bullet strike Emma.

Before she fell to the ground and died.

You'd expect me to resist the police, but I don't.

When they come for me, Richard makes a point of telling them I'm now unarmed. For all the good it does them – the private tutor is down, which means I won in one way or another. It's hard to say if Richard is going to survive this, but if he does, then this won't be the end of it. Emma is dead as a doornail, and Jacob... well, I'll get him someday.

Then we can all be together again.

The police flood into the room and pick me up off the floor. The empty rifle lies by the window, which they rush to kick away from me as if I can cause any more damage with it. What's done is done, and that's enough to keep a huge smile on my face.

As they lead me downstairs, all I see are bright red and blue lights blinking through the front of the house. There's blood everywhere – Richard's, ha ha – and they've already taken him out on a stretcher. I have no idea if he's alive or dead at this point, but I'm pretty sure he'll die soon enough. After all that blood loss, he'd better.

Outside, some of the Wedchester residents have journeyed up the hill to view the commotion. It makes me hate them even more than usual, which is saying something. Even though I'd done my best to paint my husband as the villain in all of this, it looks like I'll be taking the fall for everything that's happened. It's fair to say I'm responsible for Emma's death, but what happened to Katie is a little more complicated.

I'll keep that information in my back pocket for now.

It could prove extremely useful later.

I hang my head in shame as the townsfolk use their phones to snap pictures and videos of my arrest. There are three police cars outside – more than Wedchester has to offer, so one of them must have come from the nearest town – and an ambulance where Richard is dying. I wonder what happened to Emma in all of this. Is she in that same ambulance, or is she already away with the coroner, where she'll soon be completely forgotten?

Just like Katie was... eventually.

The two policemen with their hands on me stop beside a car. The door is open, but one of their colleagues has come to talk to them. They talk in low mumbles, which is completely drowned out by the commotion of the snooping townsfolk at my front gate.

It's not until then that I wonder where Jacob has gone. Let's face it, one of only two things could have happened: either the police have taken him somewhere safe while they figure out what to do with him, or the bullet went through Emma and got him, too. In that case, he's now wherever Emma is, which is fine by me.

Two for the price of one.

I will miss him though. Jacob was a lovely little boy. Despite his misaligned affections for his tutors, I feel like he really would have loved me if life was somewhat different. Perhaps we should have enrolled him in a public school (disgusting, I know) so he'd have more chance of socialising. Would that have made him more well rounded?

We'll never know.

The officers finish talking. One of them tells me to wait, as if I have any choice while their hands are clamped around my too-thin arms. I stand there in the cold, starting to shake while the wind musses my hair. The police turn towards the ambulance, where Richard is escorted from the rear step and towards us, off the stretcher. I try to take a step back because I don't want him anywhere near me ever again. Not unless it's because I choose it – to give me another shot at ending his life. That's what he deserves, after all.

'Your husband is a very persuasive man,' one of the officers says to me, and then they both let me go and step aside while Richard comes closer. 'It seems he'd like a word with you before we get you out of here.'

My mouth hangs open in shock. How can they allow this? I'm now exposed to the man I shot – the man I plotted to pin everything on – and there's nothing standing between us. As he steps up to me, his hand clutching a piece of gauze that he presses to his bloodstained chest, he gives me a thin, wry smile that shakes my soul.

Then, he speaks.

'I just want you to know that this isn't something you can win,' he says with a smile that looks like it takes some real effort. 'Even if I die, Jacob is going to be just fine. You're going to prison just for shooting me, and...'

Everyone around us pauses while Richard groans and bends over slightly, wincing. A paramedic rushes towards him, but he puts out a hand to stop her. She soon backs off. Anything to make sure he gets the last word. Oh, how I hate him.

'There are witnesses who saw you fire at Emma,' he finishes, exhaling painfully.

I give him my best smile, but I have to admit it's a little painted on. The idea of prison is terrifying for someone like me – someone who grew up in a somewhat privileged household. I don't want to imagine the dinners, the lack of privacy, the lack of fashion.

The lack of money.

Oh, but my life won't carry on for too much longer. I made my intentions rather clear tonight, and they're not about to change. At some point, everything is going to tip in my favour. After that... well, they'll see.

'You have nothing to say?' Richard demands. 'Nothing at all?'

'What would you like me to say?' I ask with a sneer. 'That I'm sorry? That I wish I could take back all the things that happened between us? You seem to be forgetting that the evidence is mounted up against you. The whole town knows you're controlling and abusive. They've seen the marks. Emma was the only one who knew the truth, and she's gone. Let's face it: you think you're in control, but you have nothing.'

Richard's eyes fire into me like bullets. I can tell he's stumped about what to say. To think, he came over here feeling all high and mighty, as if he's just got away with a fate worse than death. But now? Now he knows he's screwed even if he does survive.

Which isn't looking likely.

The paramedic comes forward, gently touching his back. She's a young, pretty thing but comes across as a little too stern. The face doesn't match the personality, which makes me think Richard's status is more critical than he believes.

'We really need to get you to hospital,' she says.

'Yes, I'm coming.'

Once more, she backs off, all the way to the

ambulance this time. I suppose she's aware that Richard is a doctor and that he above everyone else knows how badly he needs help. That's what makes it all the scarier that he still hasn't moved.

'There's one thing you don't know,' he says smugly, and I've never been more desperate to tear the head from his neck. Even as he takes a short, stumbling step back before regaining composure, I want to speed up the process by jabbing something into his already fatal wound.

'Yes, I'm sure there is,' I tell him, grinning because I know I've won.

'There's no way you're ever leaving that prison cell.'

I laugh at him. It's not fake but exaggerated. 'And why is that, pray tell?'

'Because there *is* somebody alive who will testify against you.'

'Right. And who might that be?'

Richard's eyes level with mine. My heart is racing, my legs ready to give out, but I set my jaw and stare back at him as if to show all the confidence in the world. Even if he is about to win, I can't let him see that. Anyway, his own confidence is starting to scare me. I want to scurry into a hole and stay there where it's safe and sound.

Piercing me through those smug, arrogant eyes, he leans in close and whispers.

'Emma,' he says. 'Emma is alive.'

Heat flushes through me. Richard turns his back on me, staggering to the ambulance. The police close in on me then, and I lose control of my senses. No point keeping up appearances now that all this evidence is mounted up against me. I lean into my rage, letting it all out in one long, explosive threat that's a long time coming.

'You're going to die, you arrogant son of a bitch! You, Jacob, and that little bitch who stood between us! It might not be now, and it might not be tomorrow, but don't forget there's one more card to play. Tell them what happened to Katie, you bastard!'

Richard does stop, but he clearly thinks better of responding. Not that it matters. The police show me into the back of the car. I could tell them the truth right now and maybe claim back some of my reputation, but that little playing card I bragged about – the wildcard that will turn this entire situation on its head – is in my back pocket.

I think about it as we drive away from the scene. Exhaustion hits me out of the blue, leaving me staring lifelessly out of the window as we pass through the small town of Wedchester. It's hard to believe that this morning I had everything, and now... what's left? A son I'll never see again? A secret only I know that will turn everything around?

Yes, that is a card I'll play soon enough.

Whenever it's most effective.

Chapter Thirty-One

THEY SAY you can't dream when you're unconscious, but I hear things.

I don't know if it's in the real world or my dream, but there's a steady beeping sound. Maybe I'm drifting out of a coma and into a light sleep as my senses are all coming back to me. There's an anaemic smell in the air, and my body is cold. Even with the weight of sheets over my body, the goosebumps prickle out of my skin. My back is suffering, as if I've slept in an uncomfortable bed for a long, long time.

But it's my stomach that hurts the most. This isn't a surface-level pain but something deep. Something *internal*. I want to reach out and touch it, but all my strength has left me. I can barely open my eyes, but I beat the odds and do it anyway.

The room is dim and cold. Depressing, really. A quick look around reveals an old, seventies-style striped décor but with a flat-screen TV from the mid-noughties. A nurse has her back to me, but when she turns, she asks how I'm feeling. I tell her I'm okay but tired, and apparently, that's to be expected. When she leaves the room, it feels like she's not coming back, but she soon returns with a half-smiling young boy at her side.

'Jacob,' I say, relieved to see him unharmed.

Without a word, he rushes forward and leans over the bed, planting a long, loving kiss on my cheek. His face is warm and comforting, but he quickly sits back in the ugly green chair beside the bed, swinging his little legs back and forth.

'This young man refuses to leave the hospital,' the nurse says. 'Even when the police tried to take him away, he insisted he be here when you wake up. You *and* him.'

The nurse points to my side, where a parallel bed looms across the room. A large man – Richard, I quickly realise – lies unconscious on his back. Much like myself, he also has an abundance of machines around him, but he also has a mask cupped over his pale face. I don't know much about modern medicine, but I'm smart enough to know what death looks like.

Richard isn't far from it.

'Don't look so serious,' the nurse says. 'He's going to be just fine.'

I sigh a breath of relief. The nurse leaves me alone with Jacob, who's smiling through his sadness. There's no fooling me – the boy's mother was just arrested after shooting his dad and then trying to kill him. That's the kind of trauma that will haunt him for years, even with the best care ahead of him. As for Richard... let's just hope he wakes up soon.

'Are you okay?' I ask, struggling to speak.

'I think so. Are you?'

'Actually, I've seen better days.'

'Does it hurt?'

'A little.'

Looking to my side, where I feel a button, I incline the bed and slowly rise to see him better. Jacob sits up straight, attentive, like he's just about to take a piano lesson. He's looking right at me like he expects me to take control, but I don't know what to say or do.

This situation is brand new to me.

'Are you still going to teach me?' he asks, giving in and taking the lead.

'Well, that depends.'

'On what?'

'Whether your dad still wants to employ me.'

Jacob's eyes blink with sadness as he looks over at his father. I can tell he's panicking about whether he'll wake up, and I want to assure him. The nurse's words offered hope, but her tone didn't. I imagine she says things like that to everyone – it's probably just compassion.

'He'll be okay, won't he?' Jacob asks.

'Let's just focus on what to do today.'

'Please just answer the question. Will Daddy wake up?'

Blowing out a stressed, exhausted breath, I roll my head to one side and get a good look at Richard. He's got so many machines around him that he looks like one himself. It's not looking good, but if I were a vulnerable young child, I'd want all the assurance I could get. That's why, when I turn back to look at him, I meet his eye and lie as best I can.

'He'll be fine,' I say with a weak smile. 'I promise.'

. . .

It turns out I was right.

Richard woke up the day after I made that promise (thank God). Until then, Jacob had been staying with Martha from the bed and breakfast. She opted to take care of him for free, and I'm sure Richard wouldn't have minded me giving my approval. Apparently, half the town knew her as a mother figure anyway, so it solved a problem.

After waking up, Richard and I spend some time together in that hospital room, forced to be roommates for the time being. I'd be lying if I said a friendship wasn't born from all this, but he still has his quiet moments. I understand completely; he's gone through so much in the past couple of days – we all have – but his pain was prefaced with years of being married to an absolute nutcase. If he knew she was going to try to kill us all, would he have stayed?

Ask him about Katie, my inner voice begs.

I shut it into the back of my mind for a better time.

It's around a week before they let us go, with only a few hours between us. Richard is free to leave, but he waits around for me in the hospital reception area. He doesn't want to go anywhere without the woman who saved his son, he says, which does make me smile. The nurse gives me a fresh bandage around my stomach wound – the stitches do the rest of the work – and I'm soon out into the fresh winter air of a hospital just outside Wedchester.

Richard keeps a hand behind me in case I fall, which I think is really sweet because his body took more of a punishment than mine did. Not by much, but enough. We stand outside those doors together, waiting for a taxi that feels like it will never come. I don't mind.

At least we get to talk one last time.

'What will you do next?' he says. 'More tutoring work?'

'It's all I'm good for.'

'Don't be so sure. You'd make a pretty good bodyguard. Just like that film.'

'Didn't Kevin Costner die in that?'

'I have no idea. It's been a long time, and I didn't like it much.'

'Great soundtrack though.'

'Hmm...'

It's too quiet out here by the front gates. There's no sign of anyone except a nurse I recognise, who's drinking a coffee out in the cold. She's huddled over her cup, and she waves, then goes inside when I wave back. She's the only sign of life out here.

'Can I ask you something?' I say to Richard.

'Anything you want.'

'If I were to stay in Wedchester a while longer, could I still work for you?'

Richard turns to me then, looking me up and down as if to search for some telling sign that I'm joking. I'm not – Jacob warmed to me pretty quickly, and I warmed to him even faster. But Richard's company is also becoming nicely familiar to me now. I don't have a whole lot of friends in the world, so sticking around might be a good idea... for now.

'That's not a good idea,' he says at long last. Richard must see my heart break because he quickly picks it back up. 'Oh no, it's not because of you. It's just that Jacob and I don't want to go back in that house for a while, so we were thinking of hitting the road. You know, a few weeks or months going wherever life takes us.'

'Won't the police find that suspicious?'

'Maybe. Should be fine though, as long as I don't leave the country.'

'But, you know... I don't have a fixed abode either.'

I turn away from Richard so he won't see the grin I'm giving off like an idiot. I can sense his smile, too, but he makes no such effort to hide it. When he clears his throat and looks away, his next words are enough to give me a little hope for the future.

'Okay,' he says. 'Then why don't you join us for a while?'

He doesn't have to ask me twice.

Two weeks pass, and we're already settled into our new lives. I know it's temporary, but this is the happiest I've been in a long time. Even if my stitches have torn twice (luckily, I have a doctor in close proximity at all times).

We've done it with a large motorhome Richard bought brand new. I thought he was just showing off his money at first, but one night, he confided in me that he's going to sell the house and start fresh on the road. If you're going to do something like that, you might as well do it in a shiny new, reliable vehicle with hot water and multiple beds.

Jacob is doing well, too. I'm being paid to keep him occupied with school routines, although I confess to giving him a break after all he's been through. It can't be easy knowing your mum is a murderous lunatic, but he's getting by. We do keep our ears to the ground about Nora, but it's... complicated. I'll explain later.

Somehow, we've ended up in a seaside town called Weston-super-Mare. Richard had never heard of it before, so I convinced him to take us down there by using the pier and amusement arcades as a lure. Jacob was excited at the mere mention of riding donkeys on the beach, and everything was looking brighter. Everything... except the sky.

I hadn't accounted for the bitter February weather, and let me tell you that nowhere is colder than a beach in those first two months of the year. After we all expressed our disappointment – and I accepted the blame – it was quickly decided that we would head somewhere less open and would return here during the summer.

Not that I'll still be here.

The length of my employment has not yet been discussed. Richard occasionally hints that he wouldn't hate having me around for as long as I'm willing to stay. I feel more optimistic about this than you might imagine. I even make a couple of hints myself because, honestly, I love their company, and I've nowhere else to go.

This is the perfect fit for me.

We soon move on to Bath, which is a gorgeous city not far from Bristol. As soon as we arrive at a campsite that's packed to the brim, Richard asks his son to occupy himself with drawing for a few minutes while he and I have a chat. Jacob merrily agrees and sits himself at the motorhome's dinner table while the adults talk outside.

That's where he tells me the latest news about Nora.

I cup a hand to my mouth, hardly able to believe what I'm hearing. Richard should be even more upset. That's his wife, after all – for better or worse, as they more than likely vowed – and now he had to consider how to tell Jacob. It wasn't an easy task, which is why I offer to be there with him while it happens.

'Are you sure?' he asks. 'You have no idea how much I'd appreciate that.'

'Of course. After all of this' – I gesture around us – 'it's the least I can do.'

We head inside to tell Jacob the news. Nora has been begging the police to reach out to Richard and arrange visitation. They weren't able to get hold of us at first (one of the downsides to being on the road while Richard tightened his no-phone rule). If it weren't for the radio, he wouldn't have even heard the news yet. He wouldn't have had to sit his son down and try not to cry. He wouldn't have to explain to a six-year-old that his mother had been killed in prison.

Jacob takes it just like you'd expect. The tears come thick and fast, and he leaps off his chair to hug his father. Richard holds him tight, his own tears coming, and I suddenly realise this isn't my place. I get up and go outside, leaving the two of them to grieve for as long as they need. It's going to take some time to heal from this one.

They'll be ready to move on soon enough, and I'm in no hurry. Life has been a whirlwind lately, so I don't mind taking a walk around this beautiful, stony city by myself. I stop for coffee there, buy a toy for Jacob that might cheer him up, then contemplate heading back to the motorhome. In time, we can all rest in the knowledge that we've had closure on everything.

Well, there is still one thing I want to know…

I'll ask when the time is right.

Chapter Thirty-Two

Eight months is enough time to grieve, right?

I hope so because Richard has just offered to take me out to dinner. By 'out', he means cooking a meal exclusively for us after Jacob has gone to bed, serving it on the fold-out picnic table that slides underneath the motorhome. His enormous house was sold a long time ago, so now he's just enjoying the money while taking some time off work. He's enjoying himself, he says, because he has no responsibilities except for getting us from one place to another and being a good dad. I have the education taken care of, which is half the battle.

Jacob is in bed by seven o'clock, taking a brand-new book with him. I'm so proud of how far along his reading is coming – not only is he ahead of average kids his age, but it's not remotely a chore for him. Even amidst all the mourning for his mother, he somehow still managed to develop all of his skills as a student.

Good for him.

Richard keeps his promise, too, following through on that meal. He's cooked us both some steaks and peppered them while serving with triple-cooked chips and a coleslaw that for some reason says 'home-made' on the tub... that he bought from a supermarket. I don't care about the quality of the food anyway. It's his company I want the most.

I'm trying not to feel guilty about being romanced by my employer. I feel like I've woven my way through a family, inserting myself and tearing them apart before declaring myself This Year's Model. It wasn't deliberate – I'm not even so sure I like Richard in that way – but when a strong, handsome, rich man with a nice personality shows an interest in you, saying no is nothing short of idiotic. As long as it doesn't affect my employment.

We talk all night, sipping wine and talking about our pasts. Richard tells me about his education that was funded by his strict parents. They passed a few years back, and Nora was there to pick up the pieces (emotionally speaking). I tell him about my background in teaching, my decision to become a private tutor, and how lucky I felt to have met him.

This, as you can imagine, led to an awkward silence. That awkward silence led to him gently brushing stray hair away from my face. My heart pulses as he stares deeply into my soul and slowly leans in for a kiss that's either going to feel very right or very wrong.

I stop it before it happens. Richard apologises profusely, but I assure him he's not the problem. Well, not technically. It's just that there's still a mystery surrounding the woman who came before me. There's no way I can enter a relationship with a man who was once accused of murder. Not without knowing the full story straight from the horse's mouth.

'Okay,' he says, backing off and nodding slowly. 'You really want to know?'

'Yes,' I tell him. 'More than anything.'

Knowing that it's the last roadblock before a happy future with just the three of us, Richard puts his wine back on the table, takes a minute to gather his thoughts, and clears his throat. Then, when he's ready, he starts to tell me his deepest, darkest secret.

All I have to do is listen.

'The first thing you have to remember,' Richard says, wringing his fingers in his lap, 'is that you should forget anything Nora ever told you about Katie. The truth is, she was a very pretty young woman who Nora became extremely jealous of from the very beginning.'

I perk up and nod, listening. Probably frowning.

'Katie showed up just like you did,' he goes on. 'She turned up out of the blue, enquiring about a job we advertised on a noticeboard in town. Everything about her seemed just right; she was qualified, a good communicator, and she got on incredibly well with Jacob. At least for the short amount of time she was teaching.

'Nora caught Katie and I chatting a couple of times. I suppose I understand why she thought we were flirting, but nothing was ever going to come of it. Especially after one day, where Katie invited me into the woods for a wander. I met her there just to tell her no, but apparently, even that looked suspicious. I did nothing wrong, however. Despite everything, I was very loyal to my wife and intended to be until the day I died. Or the day *she*...

'That's not important. The fact is, Nora started pulling her away from teaching, encouraging her to do more household-type stuff like cooking for Jacob and cleaning his bedroom. That started to become cooking for all of us and cleaning all of the rooms. Katie – bless her heart – was too kind a person to say no, getting straight on those duties so she could hurry back to teach Jacob before the day would end. Nora actually confessed to me once, when we were lying in bed, that she wanted Katie to do as much housework as possible just so she would stay away from our family. I tried telling her that was the whole point of hiring a private tutor, but she wouldn't listen to me. You know what she was like.'

I really do, but I don't want to interrupt his flow. As it turns out, Jacob stirring behind the nearby window does. Even though it's a hot summer night, Richard goes to the window and talks through the gap, telling his son he needs a few minutes of privacy. He closes the window, then comes back to me, sitting further away than he was before.

He takes a long drink of wine.

'It got worse when Katie came asking me for help. The poor girl was in tears, feeling like my wife was bullying her. She practically begged me to have words with Nora, which I felt obligated to do. You can guess how well she reacted to that.

'That was one of the few conversations I won, but that wasn't worth a thing. A few days later, Katie came to thank me for the sudden freedom she'd been granted to educate. The problem was she thanked me by kissing me on the cheek. It was pretty unprofessional, but it was too late to do anything about that.'

'Let me guess,' I say, unable to resist. 'Nora saw.'

Richard nods. 'She came charging towards Katie, shoving and screaming and all sorts. Anything short of scratching out her eyes. That was the first real sign I got that Nora was unable to control her urges. In time, that led to me placating her, giving in to her every demand. She'd proven how capable she was of hurting someone, and if Jacob ever upset her...

'Anyway, I managed to intervene on that occasion. Katie did report it to the police, but she didn't press charges. I think it was more to protect herself from future attacks than to punish Nora for the last one. Not that it did her any good. You've heard the rest.'

I watch him for a while before I say anything, as it feels like he wants me to fill in the gap – to tell the rest of the story for him. Well, I'm not going to do that, but I want to make sure we're talking about the same thing here...

'I've heard rumours, but nobody knows if they're true.'

'What have you heard?'

'That you killed Katie and got away with it.'

Richard sighs and shakes his head, his cheeks flushing scarlet. 'No. God, no. I wish it was as simple as that. At least I could solve the whole thing with a simple confession and be punished accordingly. But it's much more complicated.

'Nora spent a long time following Katie around, threatening her and telling her to leave. I did my best to assure Katie that her employment here was safe as long as she wished to remain under our employ. Even though she felt unsafe, she said she trusted me enough to keep working for a little while longer, and she also loved Jacob. They had such a good relationship.

'Katie... got in the way one day. Not of me, but

of Nora. She was supposed to be watching Jacob, but she sneaked out for a quick bathroom break. Jacob was younger at the time, so he felt somewhat more compelled to exercise his freedom. He did what most kids his age would do – jumping on the bed and running riot. Until he tripped and hurt himself.'

I grow uncomfortable in my seat, adjusting myself while I hang on Richard's every word. The scene is set, and I can tell it's getting to the big part – the juicy reveal. The answers everyone in Wedchester wanted all along. Not to mention the police.

'Nora attacked her at the top of the stairs,' he says in a wavering voice. 'I caught them right in the middle of a heated exchange, and Nora had that look in her eye again. The fiery one. I rushed into the middle to break them apart, shoving them both away from each other. Only I pushed a little too hard. Katie was... well, she fell.'

The table area goes quiet. I don't fill the silence.

'She went all the way down the stairs. I'll spare you the details about the bumps and bruises, but when she finally landed at the bottom, she was almost dead. Her injuries were too severe, and it's hard to say if she'd have made it. I guess you could say I killed her, but...'

A shake of his head. 'I didn't mean to do it. I wanted to help her, but Nora followed me down the stairs. She must have gone into the kitchen – I didn't see her go in, but she came out with a knife that she used to finish Katie off. I've never seen anything like it, Emma. My own wife, the woman I loved, so eager to plunge that knife into Katie's chest. Multiple times.

'There was no saving her then. We had a future to think about. Jacob needed both his parents, but we'd both committed murder. Now, you can argue the murder versus manslaughter thing all day long, but I had plenty of chances to report it. To come forward.'

'Why didn't you?' I ask, everything I know about this man quickly disappearing. 'You could have put the whole thing on Nora. Then Jacob would still have his father around. It's exactly the situation you're in now, except we wouldn't have gone through everything we did.'

'Nora would have told,' he says. 'It's lucky she didn't before she was killed.'

I sort of agree, but there's no more to say on the matter. I just let him continue.

'Nora panicked. She insisted I took Katie's body deep into the woods. We stayed up all night, taking it in turns to dig so we could get her at least six feet under. As soon as it was done, I just wanted to go inside and cry, but Nora made me promise never to say a word. If I did, she was going to walk right into Jacob's bedroom and kill him, too. I was never certain she would do it, but I didn't want to take the chance and...'

Richard bursts into tears. I don't know what to say. I understand the situation, but this is more from a viewer's perspective. Like I'm watching it on a TV show and shouting my advice from the comfort of an armchair. It's no big shock to hear that Katie died – I'm not even that surprised to hear Richard was partly responsible, but to see him break down like this...

I shift along the seat and put my arms around him. There's so much to do with this information that I don't know where to start. Although having him in my arms brings him one step closer to what he needs from me. And not just what he needs.

But what he deserves.

I HAVE A CONFESSION TO MAKE.

The Private Tutor

Never have I lied to you – not once have I told you a mistruth. Everything you've just read is one hundred per cent honest, although I did miss out a few important details. Not the ones you'd expect either. I guess they call it a twist for a reason.

I'll start with my childhood. It was normal, just like I said. We really were close as a family, and we really did drift apart after our parents' divorce. My sister and I were devastated, and although we didn't stay in close proximity, we only had each other.

I was so shocked when I heard she'd disappeared. Apparently, a man in Wedchester had been interviewed after she mysteriously vanished. A doctor named Richard, who lived at the top of a hill with his wife and son. It didn't take any persuasion – I got right on the next bus to that miserable little town and started poking around.

The rest, as you know, is history.

Like I said, it was all true. I really do love Jacob to pieces, and Richard really is a good guy. All I ever wanted was to get some closure on my sister. Now that I know she died – that Richard and Nora worked together to cover up their mistake – I need some time to process it. If I don't, I'm likely to act on my emotions. My swirling, incomparable rage that's flaring around my head and telling me to do something stupid.

That's why I slide over to Richard. Not to hug him.

But to do what I came here to do.

After Nora killed herself, I had nothing to do but follow Richard around the country. It was the only way to get my answers. I also started carrying a penknife in my pocket because it would be foolish to trust this family after everything that's happened.

Right now, with Richard sobbing in my arms at the horrendous thing he did, I'm faced with a choice: do I forgive him and sail off into the sunset with him and his son, or do I punish him for taking away the only family who ever bothered to call in the past few years?

The decision makes itself. It's like I'm on autopilot, unable to steer my own body.

'This is for Katie... my sister,' I whisper.

Richard doesn't even get to speak before the knife plunges into his back. I hate the feeling of metal piercing flesh – of scraping against ribs as Richard expels a shocked breath down my neck. I hold him upright, regret burning through me while

I let him die in my arms. It's not hateful. It's just right. That's what I tell myself, anyway.

At some point, I'll have to let him go. Jacob will need a guardian, and there's no telling if they'll let me take over. I'll try my best because that kid truly deserves a good future. It's not his fault he was wrapped up in all this – it's his parents', and it's mine. That's why I'm going to do everything in my power to cover up this murder and keep him.

It's the least he deserves.

For other books by AJ Carter, visit:

www.ajcarterbooks.com/books

About the Author

AJ Carter is a psychological thriller author from Bristol, England. His first book, *The Family Secret*, is praised by critics around the world, and he continues to regularly deliver suspenseful novels you can't put down.

Sign up to his mailing list today and be the first to hear about upcoming releases and hot new deals for existing books. You'll also receive a FREE digital copy of *The Couple Downstairs* – an unputdownable domestic thriller you won't find anywhere else in the world.

www.ajcarterbooks.com/subscribe

Printed in Great Britain
by Amazon